THE BURYING PLACE

VICKY JONES
CLAIRE HACKNEY

Copyright © 2020 by Vicky Jones

All rights reserved.

No part of this book may be reproduced in any form or by any electronic or mechanical means, including information storage and retrieval systems, without written permission from the author, except for the use of brief quotations in a book review.

Acknowledgments

Special mention to crime author Mark Romain for all the police procedural advice and input.

Visit his website:
www.markromain.com

Contents

Join in!	vii
About Vicky Jones	ix
About Claire Hackney	xi
The DI Rachel Morrison series	xiii
The DI Rachel Morrison series	xv
Also by Vicky Jones and Claire Hackney	xvii
Also by Vicky Jones and Claire Hackney	xix
Also by Vicky Jones and Claire Hackney	xxi
Also by Vicky Jones and Claire Hackney	xxiii
Chapter 1	1
Chapter 2	14
Chapter 3	21
Chapter 4	28
Chapter 5	33
Chapter 6	41
Chapter 7	48
Chapter 8	51
Chapter 9	59
Chapter 10	63
Chapter 11	71
Chapter 12	93
Chapter 13	106
Chapter 14	117
Chapter 15	125
Chapter 16	132
Chapter 17	145
Chapter 18	153
Chapter 19	163
Chapter 20	172
Chapter 21	178
Chapter 22	191
Chapter 23	197

Epilogue	203
FREE FIRST CHAPTER FOR YOU!	209
Prologue	211
The DI Rachel Morrison series	215
The DI Rachel Morrison series	217
Also by Vicky Jones and Claire Hackney	219
Also by Vicky Jones and Claire Hackney	221
Also by Vicky Jones and Claire Hackney	223
Also by Vicky Jones and Claire Hackney	225
Join in!	227
Acknowledgments	229
Our Team	231

Join in!

If you would like to receive regular behind-the-scenes updates, get beta reading opportunities, enter giveaways and much, much more, simply visit the site below:

http://hackneyandjones.com

About Vicky Jones

Vicky Jones was born in Essex, England. She is an author and singer-songwriter, with numerous examples of her work on iTunes and YouTube. At 20 years old she entered the Royal Navy. After leaving the Navy realising she was drifting through life with no sense of direction, she wrote a bucket list of 300 things to achieve which took her traveling, facing her fears and going for her dreams. At the time of printing, she is two-thirds of the way through her bucket list.

One item on her list was to write a song for a cause. Her anti-bullying track called "House of Cards" is now on iTunes to download.

Writing a novel was on her bucket list, and through a chance writing competition at her local writing group, the idea for *Meet Me At 10* was born. Vicky hopes she can change hearts and minds due to some of the gritty themes of the book.

Vicky is a keen traveler, stemming from her days traveling the world in the Royal Navy, and has visited around 50 countries so far. She has also graduated from The Open University after studying part time for her degree in psychology and criminology—another bucket list tick! She is currently writing a book series about her bucket list adventures, the first of which is entitled *'Project Me, Project You'*, alongside planning and writing more fiction books and book marketing guides for self-published authors.

Also in the pipeline is a writing course, put together to help aspiring authors plan and write their first novel.

She now lives in Cheshire, splitting her time between there and visiting her family and friends back in Essex.

For more information on upcoming book releases, to tell us what you think of the books, or just to say hi, visit the sites below:

facebook.com/VickyJonesWriter
twitter.com/vickyjones7
instagram.com/vickytjones

About Claire Hackney

Claire Hackney is a former English Literature, Drama and Media Studies teacher who, after attending a local writing group with Vicky and writing several of her own short stories over the years, has now decided to focus her career on full-time novel writing.

She is an avid historian and has thoroughly enjoyed researching different aspects of the 1950s for the 'Shona Jackson' trilogy of novels.

Claire is very much looking forward getting started on the many future writing projects she and Vicky have in the pipeline, including the 'DI Rachel Morrison' thriller series and several standalone novels.

For more information on upcoming book releases, to tell us what you think of the books, or just to say hi, visit the sites below:

facebook.com/ClaireHackneyAuthor
twitter.com/clairehac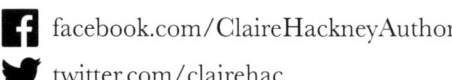
instagram.com/clairehackneyauthor

The DI Rachel Morrison series

The Nurse. The Teacher. The Gardener.

You have motive. You have means. Do you take the opportunity? Three innocent people from completely different walks of life are presented with an impossible decision. DOWNLOAD FREE: www.hackneyandjones.com

The DI Rachel Morrison series

Book 2: We Don't Speak About Mollie

What if everybody knew what you did, except you? Seconded up from Cornwall to a Task Force in Liverpool, DI Rachel Morrison has a mysterious case brought to her. Haunted by her past, Katie Spencer seeks answers, but a familiar face tells her a story that completely destroys her world. Together with DI Morrison, Katie pieces together the fragments of her memory. But is knowing the truth a blessing or a curse? And just who exactly is Mollie?

Also by Vicky Jones and Claire Hackney

Chloe - A prequel to Meet Me at 10

What if a life-shattering family tragedy forces you to completely rethink your future? Destined for a different path in life, twenty-year-old Chloe Bruce's world is shattered after a tragic accident on her father's plantation in Alabama. Suddenly thrust into the limelight, as the new heir to the Bruce family business, she is sent off to university to study and equip herself with the knowledge needed to succeed her father. But not everything in life can be learned from a textbook, as Chloe realises when she meets Mia… DOWNLOAD FREE: www.hackneyandjones.com

Also by Vicky Jones and Claire Hackney

Shona: Book 1 - A prequel to Meet Me at 10

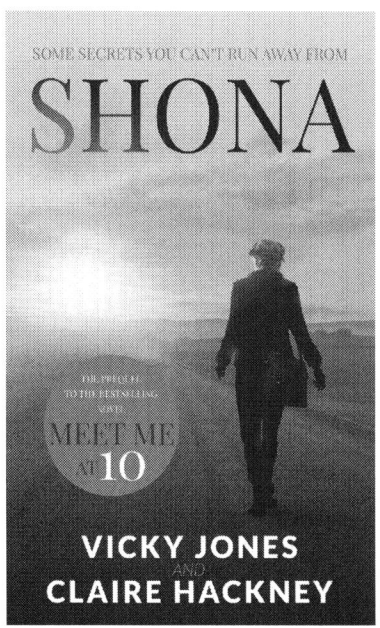

Everyone has a secret. Hers could get her killed…
Mississippi, 1956. Shona Jackson knows two things —how to repair cars and that her dark childhood secret must stay buried. On the run from Louisiana, she finds shelter in the home of a kindly old lady and a job as a mechanic. But a woman working a man's job can't avoid notice in a small town. And attention is dangerous…

Also by Vicky Jones and Claire Hackney

Meet Me At 10: Book 2

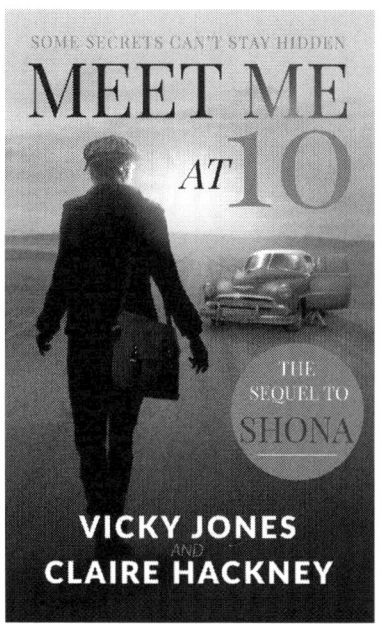

Four lives inextricably linked. Will tragic events part them forever? Shona Jackson is on the run again, forced to flee Mississippi. Arriving in Alabama, to continue her journey to safety, she convinces Jeffrey Ellis, the wealthy co-owner of a machinery plant, to give her a job. But when Chloe Bruce returns from college and is introduced to the workforce, there are devastating consequences for all those involved.

Also by Vicky Jones and Claire Hackney

The Beach House: Book 3

New town. New life. Old enemies. With the past and present colliding and threatening their future together, can Shona protect her new life and the lives of those closest to her?

THE BURYING PLACE

Chapter 1

"Don't fuck this up, Rachel," Superintendent Elaine Hargreaves warned as she walked up towards her senior investigating officer, Detective Inspector Rachel Morrison. She brushed off a piece of lint caught in the crown badge on her epaulette and straightened her black and white checked cravat. The atmosphere in the cramped room was getting tenser by the second, as the swathes of news reporters clamoured for the prized seats nearest the front. A long table had been put against the wall near the back door to the room and behind it stood four chairs waiting to be occupied. Four glasses of water sat next to four long, thin microphone stands being tested by a technician. The news reporters chatted to each other, while each camera crew with them adjusted their camera settings and checked their flashes were ready.

"No, ma'am, of course not," Rachel replied, taking a sip from her takeaway coffee. Now in her late thirties, she had been a detective for nearly ten years, and press conferences were not her favourite part of the job. She swept a lock of long, dark brown hair away from her brow and smoothed down the front of her smart navy blue slim-fit trouser suit. "Cornwall's finest in this morning, I see, ma'am?"

"Not just the locals. National news are here as well. Look."

Hargreaves nodded in the direction of a group of reporters who had pulled rank and sat in the front row, much to the annoyance of the tutting group from the Falmouth Packet. "Same old vultures, looking for their front-page headline," Hargreaves added, pursing her lips and scanning her ice-blue eyes across the room. She was in her early fifties, well built, with a mop of short dark, almost black hair, slightly curly on the top. Squinting as a flash went off in her direction, reflecting against the shiny silver buttons on her police uniform, Hargreaves turned back to face Rachel, her expression set hard. "You need to get results on this one, ASAP. I'm getting enough shit over normal people disappearing off the face of the earth as it is, without rich widows going missing now too."

"Understood, ma'am. Once we get the press conference out of the way we can get cracking. That's the daughter over there. Amanda. She seems in shock still."

Rachel nodded towards a young, brown-haired girl, around twenty-four years old, who had just walked in through the back room door. She was around five feet five tall and wearing a fitted purple hoodie and blue stonewashed jeans. She sat down in the middle left chair and took a sip of water. Eyes lowered, she looked around the room and breathed in deeply. Taking a seat next to Amanda at the long table flanked by the reporters and a throng of crew from *Cornwall Live* was another girl, of similar age, slightly smaller build and wearing a neatly pressed navy blue shirt and smart black trousers. She wore her light brown hair tied back in a tight ponytail and had large horn-rimmed glasses perched on her long beaky nose.

"No other family?" Hargreaves remarked, noticing the panel was sparse.

"Just an uncle. Father died ten years ago. That's her friend." Rachel checked her notepad. "Poppy."

Moments after Amanda whispered in Poppy's ear, Poppy reached down into her handbag and pulled out a small packet of tissues. Handing her one, her friend draped a comforting arm around Amanda as she dabbed at her eyes.

"Right, well, looks like we're good to go," Hargreaves said, catching the nod from the communications officer. A uniformed police constable sat on the seat next to Poppy. "Results, DI Morrison. That's what I want." Hargreaves flashed Rachel a sharp stare before walking away, leaving Rachel to take occupancy of the last remaining seat at the table.

———

"Diana Walker, from the Kynance Cove area of Mount's Bay, Cornwall, has been missing for four days now, so it's safe to say everyone who knows her and cares for her is very concerned for her wellbeing. Diana is fifty-nine years old, average height, slim build, with shoulder length brown hair and brown eyes. She was last seen leaving her home on the morning of Thursday, April eleventh. Her disappearance is totally out of character and nobody has heard from her since. She hasn't used her phone or her bank cards. We are appealing to you to help us with our enquiries as every moment Diana is missing is causing heartache to her only daughter, sat next to me here."

Rachel looked over at Amanda, who licked her lips and opened her mouth to speak. As she did so a haze of camera flashes made her recoil. Regaining her composure after a hand squeeze from Poppy, Amanda began her speech, her hoarse voice barely above a whisper.

"My name is Amanda Walker. My mother has been missing for four days now. Apart from Poppy here, she's all I have in the world." She paused to hold up a photograph of her mother to the cameras, which clicked and flashed as she continued after dabbing her eyes with the same scrunched up tissue from before. "Please, if you know anything about where she may be, if you think you might have seen her or know anything at all, please call the police."

Amanda looked sideways at Rachel, who smiled. Rachel continued the address to the camera. After reading out the essentials of how to contact the police with information, she wrapped up the press conference and thanked everyone for attending.

"You did really well. That was so tough," Poppy said, hugging Amanda and clasping her hands in hers as the reporters started to leave the room. "We'll find her, I promise."

"Well done, Amanda. I know that can't have been easy," Rachel chipped in, walking up next to them. "But hopefully we can get some good leads now to find your mum."

Amanda forced back a weary smile. "Thank you, detective. I can't believe nobody knows anything. Someone must have seen her or know where she is."

Rachel nodded and rested a hand on Amanda's shoulder. "We're checking everything. Maybe Poppy here could take you home and sit with you for a while? I promise I'll call you if there are any developments."

Poppy rubbed Amanda's shoulder and smiled. "Of course I will. I'll nip out to the library later too. My boss has let me use the photocopier so I can print out some more posters of your mum. Maybe we can pin them up around town later?" She paused. "If you feel up to it, that is?"

"You're such a good friend, Poppy. What would I do without you?" Amanda replied, squeezing her hand.

Rachel smiled. The constable from the table sidled up behind her.

"That's OK. I obviously caught the boss on a good day," Poppy joked.

After seeing them off, Rachel turned to the constable. "Michelle, what did Hargreaves say? Did we impress?"

"You mean not 'fuck it up'?" PC Michelle Barlow replied, grinning and hooking the thumb of one hand on her utility belt. Her other held her police issue Sillitoe striped bowler hat. She had just turned thirty, and had long reddish-brown hair tied up in a neat bun at the back of her head. They began walking towards the door out of the appeal room and down the flagstone steps to the main entrance. "She's doing that thing where she's happy but won't let her haggard old brick-face show it."

"I'll take that for now. Can you drive us back? I need to make a few calls on the way." Rachel tossed over the keys to Michelle.

"Sure."

After Rachel had made the last of her routine calls to local bus and train stations to ask them to be on the lookout, she sat back in her seat and exhaled at length.

"So, is it a disappearance then? Or something more sinister, do you think?" Michelle asked, turning from the car park onto the road back to Lizard.

"Not sure yet. I can't see it being linked to the other disappearances around here though. She's nothing like those others. A doctor, a teacher, and a businesswoman. Now a rich widow? What kind of kidnapper has an m.o. that covers that wide a spread of individuals?" Rachel replied. She began drumming her fingers on the inside of the door.

"Hmmm…I know. It's different, this latest one, but somehow the same. All disappeared without a trace. But the town will want answers, so we need to get right on this."

"Who's the SIO here?" Rachel said with a smile.

"Sorry, boss. Just got a bit excited there, didn't I? Guess the first coffee's on me now, huh?"

Rachel crossed the large, bustling open plan area that made up the station's main CID office to a row of partitioned offices at the far end. These cubbyholes housed the station's various DIs and their immediate boss, DCI Parker. After sitting down at her cluttered desk, Rachel began flicking through her notebook. Michelle had continued on over to the small adjoining kitchenette to make good on her promise.

Minutes later, she stood at Rachel's desk holding two mugs of coffee.

"We've got to start talking to people around town on this one, Shell. Something doesn't feel right about it, and Hargreaves is up my arse already to get it boxed off," Rachel said, taking a mug from Michelle and blowing the steam off it. As if mentioning her name had conjured her up from thin air, Superintendent Hargreaves marched over to Rachel's office, her foul mood as obvious as usual.

"DI Morrison, my office. Now."

"That woman needs to get laid," Michelle muttered before returning to her own desk.

Once inside the office, Rachel took up the last remaining vacant seat. Seated around her were the station's other detective inspectors and DCI Parker. There was also the uniformed chief inspector of operations and all the shift inspectors, apart from a couple who were either doing night duty or on leave. Rachel groaned inwardly. She had forgotten about the weekly meeting, in which all the station's senior supervisors met to discuss crime trends and statistics, performance issues and any high profile cases that might require resources allocated to them.

Hargreaves sat in her brown leather chair behind her desk. "Right, everyone, welcome. DCI Parker, you and your team start us off, please."

Rachel zoned out while DCI Parker and the Ops Chief Inspector discussed budgets, crime trends and the allocation of resources, after which the shift inspectors gave their input on the latest critical incidents they had dealt with. She half-heartedly listened to DI James Cooper, the head of proactive crime, spout out a load of blarney about how the units under his command, the robbery, crime and drug squads, were all meeting their quota for arrests and stop and search, and executing search warrants at known drug addresses and making respectable seizures of Class A, B and C drugs. She listened to DI Thomas whinge about the various personnel issues he had to contend with on the units under his purview. Rachel felt some sympathy; the Crime Management Unit and Telephone Reporting Bureau were mainly staffed by officers on restricted duties due to illness or injury, those who had been gated and were forbidden to meet the public because of ongoing complaints, and part timers. At least DI Thomas had the Divisional Intelligence Unit under his command, so he was able to brag about *their* successes.

Then it was Rachel's turn. Rachel was the DI in charge of investigating reactive crime. That gave her the Beat Crimes Unit, the burglary and robber squads and, most important of all, the Main Office, who dealt with all major crime allegations within the Operational Command Unit. To the assembled group in front of her, she outlined all the ongoing cases and flagged up some budgetary issues; the lack of money to pay for overtime was hampering investigations and putting undue pressure on her detectives, some of whom were carrying as many as thirty crimes each. DCI Parker shut her down on that—'everyone was in the same boat', he pointed out brusquely. It was the government cutbacks, austerity and all that, so there was no point in moaning about it.

Finally, Hargreaves asked Rachel to talk them through the series of mispers she was investigating, the latest of which was Mrs. Walker.

"Well, ma'am, we think that Mrs. Walker's disappearance is just the latest in a long line. The doctor that went missing six months ago, Jerry Carter, left town after a difficult shift at the hospital where one of his patients died. He'd been to the funeral earlier that day as he was very close to this young girl, a cancer sufferer apparently, so it seems plausible that he would want a few days away. The next, Ryan Saunders, was a teacher at the local high school who appeared to have suffered a nervous breakdown after taking on the new role of head of year. All the strain that came with that must have taken its toll so he also wanted to disappear for a bit. The other misper was a businesswoman with a history of anxiety and depression."

DCI Parker frowned and looked around the table. DI Cooper and DI Thomas gave him a knowing look.

"What?" Hargreaves barked. She drummed her stubby fingers on the desk and glared around the room. "Am I missing an opinion you all have on this here?"

The DCI continued. "There is a suspicion that these missing persons may have decided to…" he paused and glanced around the group again. "Take their own lives. If the coastguard finds them washed up at the bottom of Lizard Point, we'll know for sure. But it's been six months now since the first disappearance, so it's unlikely. Most of us think they simply left town to have a break from what was getting them down."

"Rachel?" Hargreaves said, her icy stare laser-beamed on to her. "What are your thoughts?"

"It's possible they left town. I think we need to investigate further on this case, though. With Diana Walker there is nothing that would suggest she felt in any way she wanted to leave town. Or throw herself off Lizard Point. She has a loving daughter and lots of friends in the area. Yes, the anniversary of her husband's death is coming up, but he died over ten years ago now, so why this year would she decide to end it all? No, that doesn't seem to fit. I think this one is different. Amanda is the only one, out of all the other mispers' next of kin, who pushed us for a press conference. She's adamant something bad has happened to her mother. And I happen to think she might be right."

A groan rumbled around the table and all eyes glared at Rachel.

"You're just making extra work for yourself, going down that path," DI Thomas grumbled through his bushy white moustache.

"It's always gotta be *something* with you, Morrison," DCI Parker added, folding his arms over his portly belly. "You know that in most cases the most obvious answer is the right one. People go missing all the time. They just drop off the grid or find a quiet place to top themselves. It's Lizard, for fuck's sake, not bloody Midsomer Murders."

Prick, Rachel said in her head.

Hargreaves, in the five years of working with Rachel, had never known Rachel to ignore her copper's hunch and, being Parker's boss, decided to ignore his annoyance. "Right, fine. I think that this might be worth a little poke, but no more than that. Continue your enquiries for now, Rachel. But I can't spare another detective on this case, if it *is* even a case. My resources are already stretched to breaking point, so PC Barlow can assist you, as you two work well together. But I want this wrapped up ASAP, understood? We can't spare any more resources. For now, to the public it's just a missing person's case, understood? Dismissed."

Everyone stood up from the table and gathered their notepads up. Rachel headed back to her desk and updated Michelle, leaving out the bickering and backstabbing from her fellow DIs and DCI Parker.

"Looks like you're stuck with me on this one," Michelle said, grinning.

"Couldn't think of anyone better," Rachel replied, sitting down. "By the way, have we had anything from the tip line yet?"

Michelle put down her coffee on the end of Rachel's desk and took out her notebook. "Well, let's see." She licked a finger and leafed through the pages. "One caller thinks we should get Scott and Bailey down here sharpish, as they will solve it in no time," she said, rolling her eyes. "Or Columbo. And Drunk Dave called, swears it's something to do with 'the lights' again."

Rachel leaned her chin on her palm. "He still going on about that?"

"Says 'they are on the water'. He's adamant that when he looks out to sea the lights bounce off the water, then disappear. Unfortunately, it seems to be every time he comes out of the Anchor Pub on Lizard Point after last orders." Michelle gave a knowing smile. "Who knows, maybe Diana Walker was abducted by aliens, like everyone else who's fallen off the grid these last few months, and Dave was right all along." She took a long slurp of coffee as Rachel stifled a bored laugh. "Well, I, for one, am happy Hargreaves chose me to help you on this one."

"Stolen bins not doing it for you anymore?" Rachel said.

"Funnily enough, no. Not exactly why I joined the force. I'm serious. Anything you need, just say. I agree with you, this one just doesn't feel the same as the others that have gone missing."

"I know."

"How did Diana Walker's husband die?"

"Topped himself. Was a drinker, apparently," Rachel replied.

"Shame. All that money and it still didn't make him happy. A lesson there." Michelle's brow creased. "I reckon it could have been kidnap. If she was minted then there might be a ransom demand coming."

"Kynance Cove is famous for its towering rock stacks, green clifftops, golden sands and turquoise water. It isn't exactly known for any mafia connections, Michelle," Rachel said. "But it's a line of enquiry we'll have to follow. More likely she's been bumped off. She pissed anyone off lately?"

"Not that I've heard. She was reported to be a bit snooty, but generally friendly."

"I'm just not buying that she's fucked off somewhere," Rachel said, returning to her piles of paperwork and trying to find some order with it. She paused and set her lips. "And not to tell anyone? Not even her daughter?"

"I wouldn't tell anybody either, though. But that's 'cos I don't like people," Michelle replied.

"She's not exactly the spontaneous type either. Not according to her daughter. She plans everything in her diary, and even her window cleaner gets cancellation messages, so Amanda reckons. Her diary has upcoming hairdresser appointments so it doesn't seem she's planned to go away," Rachel said, rustling through notes and interview transcripts.

Michelle leaned in. "Maybe she's got a secret fella?"

"I knew I could rely on you for helpful suggestions," Rachel replied, a sarcastic look on her face.

"Maybe he's married. That's why she couldn't tell her daughter. Oooh, the scandal."

Rachel shook her head. "She hasn't used her mobile phone, drawn out any money or spoken to her friends or daughter."

"Well, would *you* brag about an illicit affair? Maybe she carries cash, and not an awful lot of fifty-nine-year-old women have their mobile phones up their arse all the time. Battery could have died while she was shagging all day and night in an expensive hotel and she probably forgot her phone charger."

"So, she's just lying low while she enjoys a steamy affair on the anniversary of her husband's death?" Rachel mused.

"I don't know. It might be that she decided to end it and we've not found the body yet, but that's not ringing true to me. She seems the kind of person that would leave a note." She paused and sighed.

Rachel thought about that for a moment then smiled. "Well, thank you, *detective*. I assure you I am open to every possible angle on this case and I will be looking at the details very carefully."

"Yeah? While I'm looking at my shitty homemade lunch over there and wondering why I bother trying to be healthy when it tastes like cardboard."

―――

AFTER FIVE HOURS of having her head in paperwork, Rachel looked up to see Superintendent Hargreaves walk by the door to her office. Hargreaves had a fierce reputation of keeping her workforce in line with an iron fist. Catching Michelle's eye across the room, they both forced a smile at their superior.

Rachel got up and walked over to Michelle's desk. Although the PC had a desk of her own over in Beat Crimes, where she normally worked while she gathered the evidence and experience she needed to pass the DC exams, she had virtually moved into Rachel's cramped office since she had been seconded to the misper enquiry.

"I've gone through everything we've picked up so far and, truthfully, we ain't got shit. And if it stays this way, we're fucked. Hargreaves is on the warpath wanting a quick turnaround on this one."

Michelle leaned back in her swivel chair. "Well, maybe the answer will magically appear at the bottom of a gin and tonic. What do you say? I'm buying."

"No. I need to get home. But thanks," Rachel replied.

"Adam can't survive making dinner for himself, no?"

"Something like that. Men, eh?"

"I give up with them. They do my head in. Always smell of something. Guilt usually," Michelle said.

"Right, I'm off then. See you tomorrow."

"See you tomorrow, boss."

―――――

"Hi Rachel, the usual?" the owner of the chip shop on the high street said, his rosy red cheeks illuminating his rotund, sweaty face.

"Hi Tony. Just for me, thanks. Adam isn't hungry tonight," Rachel replied, placing her handbag on the counter.

"Oh, that's a shame. What's say I put some extra chips in for you, just in case he feels up for it later?" Tony said, wiping his hands down his apron. Rachel nodded her appreciation.

―――――

Walking into her dark kitchen, Rachel flicked the light on and wrinkled her nose at the sight that greeted her. Takeaway boxes, similar to the one she was holding, were stacked in the corner by the sink, the bin overflowing with chip papers. Unable to find a clean glass in her cupboard, she settled for drinking from the can she'd got in her meal deal and walked into her front room. After flicking on the TV, she moved a pile of clean but unfolded washing from the end of the couch and plonked herself down, rummaging underneath for the remote control which had found its way between the cushions. She flicked through the hundreds of channels, nothing about them interesting her. With a rerun of *Location, Location, Location* decided upon, she picked at her fish supper, feeding most of the scraps to her black and white cat, Pickles, who'd jumped into her lap at the smell of cod wafting in the stale air.

Putting her unfinished dinner on the floor for Pickles to nibble through, Rachel checked her phone. No new messages. For the fifth time that week, she sent the same message.

`Please come home, Adam. We can talk about it. I miss you xx.`

Chapter 2

"You reckon old ma' Walker's been bumped off then, guv?" PC Jackson from the Beat Crimes Unit piped up from his desk as Rachel passed by on the way to her office the following morning. He grinned at her as he chewed messily through a bacon roll, the buttons on his crumpled white shirt straining to contain his belly.

Rachel stopped. "Not sure yet, but when we do know I'll be sure not to have you break the news to her grieving daughter, eh? And do up that top button, sharpish."

Jackson sat up straight in his chair and saw to his button, suitably told off. He lowered his eyes in embarrassment as Rachel walked away.

Sinking down into her office chair, she rubbed her eyes and yawned.

"Late night?" Michelle asked, placing Rachel's coffee cup down in front of her.

"I couldn't sleep. Kept thinking over this case. Diana Walker's been missing for nearly a week now. Hargreaves is watching my every move wanting results." She took a slow sip from her coffee. "Anything new from the tips line yet?"

"Nope. Nothing worth following up"

"Where are we with the CCTV requisition?"

"Jackson's following that up now."

Rachel looked over at him to see him trying to wipe bacon grease off his black police tie. "Great."

Poppy was busy sticking missing posters up in the front window of the town centre library.

"You're such a good friend to that girl, Poppy," her boss said, appearing behind her. She shook her head, making her grey permed hair bobble. "Even though it's a friendship I've never really understood."

"What do you mean, Margaret?" Poppy replied, turning to face her.

"Well, if you don't mind me saying, dear, you both are complete opposites. You're such a quiet girl. And that Amanda, well…" Margaret raised her eyebrows.

"What?" Poppy said, folding her arms. Her face shot a look of defence.

"She likes the high life, doesn't she? Cocktails and wild nights out, so I heard."

"Not since her mother went missing. And what if she did? Nothing wrong with that." She pushed her glasses back on her nose and squinted. "Sometimes I like doing that too. We're not that different."

"I've never seen you drunk in the eight years you've worked here, Poppy." Margaret leaned in to her. "You don't have to pretend to me, love."

"I just need to finish putting these up, then I'll start on the returns box. Was there anything else?" Poppy snapped, then regretted it.

"Well, I did want to talk to you about whether you had any ideas. You see, the library might be closing down. There was talk of it at last week's rotary meeting."

"What? Why?" Poppy replied, her eyes wide.

"Cuts. We're only a little place, in a small village. The tourists only come in here for their local maps and to find out where the best picnic spots are down the coastal path. And everyone seems to be on that Amazon site these days. No one *borrows* physical books anymore. But, the council said if we can think of ways to promote the library, and all of the other services we offer, then we might have a chance at staying open. I know you're much better with things like that than I am, so I was hoping you might be able to think of something." Margaret fiddled with the little brown buttons on her white cardigan.

"Sure, I'll have a think. Don't worry, I'm sure between us we'll convince the council how vital having a local library is. It's much more than books. Way more. People meet people in here. It's sometimes their only trip out in a week. And we have the book club, don't forget."

"Oh, thank you, Poppy. You really are an angel." Margaret clasped her wrinkly hands to her chest and beamed.

"How about a competition? Or a giveaway?"

Margaret's face sank a little. "Well, we don't really have much money for that, but nice thinking."

"OK, well, as soon as I'm done here I'll type up a petition and start collecting signatures. I'm sure there are loads of people who want us to stay open. Don't you worry."

"What are you doing here?" Amanda said, wiping the sleep out of her eye. She leaned her arm against the open front door of her mother's detached house. It was an imposing sight at the end of a gated driveway, with its slate grey bricks and Cornish stone mullion windows reflecting the late afternoon sun.

"Didn't think you'd be in the mood for cooking dinner, so I brought a pizza." Poppy held out the box.

"Oh, OK. You'd best come in then."

Poppy's grin faded at Amanda's less than overwhelming greeting. Realising this, Amanda reached out for her.

"I'm sorry, Pops, I just woke up so I'm a little groggy. Eyes just adjusting to the light and all." She pulled her through the door. "That better be pepperoni."

"Like I'd get you anything else?" Poppy said, swishing past Amanda and into the expensively decorated living room. The ornate wallpaper was white and gold striped, matching the scatter cushions and soft furnishings. Sitting on a steam cleaned and perfectly white, thick carpet, there were two large, white leather couches in an L-shape and a huge oval shaped glass coffee table in the middle of the room. Above them, in the centre of the ceiling, hung a gold filigree chandelier. "Your Instagram has gone crazy since the press conference. Have you seen it?" Poppy said, sinking onto the couch and opening up the pizza box. Poppy waited for Amanda to sit also and encouraged her to take a slice. After watching her bite into it, albeit unenthusiastically, she smiled and took a slice for herself.

"Not really looked," Amanda said in a quiet voice. She put the half eaten slice on the open lid of the box and sighed. "Sorry, mate. Not had much of an appetite these last few days."

"That's OK, it's to be expected."

"I think the police are much better placed to deal with it than Instagram, don't you? It's a space for weirdos and trolls. You should read some of the messages I get. Don't need that on top of everything else." She picked the slice back up, picked off a piece of pepperoni and nibbled at it.

"I've been out today putting more posters up around town. Someone must know something," Poppy said.

Amanda gave a wry smile. "Did your moody old boss not mind you using company time and resources doing that? I don't want you getting into trouble on my account."

"No, not at all. She's alright, you know. She's just a bit antsy about the library maybe closing. It's so crap. It's the only job I've ever loved doing." Poppy's eyes dimmed, then lit up. "Who knows, if I manage to drum up enough support to keep it open they might even promote me. Assistant manager has a good ring to it, don't you think?" Poppy looked over at Amanda whose eyes had glazed over. "Mand?"

"Hmm? Oh sorry, Pops. Yeah, hopefully. You deserve it. You're amazing at making things happen."

"I've started a Find Diana Walker page on Facebook. With your following, I'm sure we'll get loads of shares."

"You're such a good friend, Pops. I'm lucky to have you."

"I learned all my tricks from you, remember? Social media queen over there," Poppy said. "I know you'd be doing the same if your head wasn't all over the place."

"You got that right. Mum went out, then never came back." She wiped a tear. "How fucked up is that? Where is she, Poppy?"

Poppy shrugged. "Has Max been round to stay yet? I hate you being alone in this big house. Especially if your mum might have been abducted."

Amanda leaned back into the couch cushions. "You know I don't like guys staying over too soon. It's only been six weeks since we got together. Anyway, he doesn't like leaving that dog of his overnight, so it suits him too. Obsessed over that thing, he is. He did send those flowers over there though." She nodded towards a huge bouquet on the solid oak sideboard.

"Maybe you could go see your therapist again? Talk all this through with him. It can't be easy on your own. I mean, you've always got me, but maybe an expert to talk to would be good?"

"I've finished all my sessions now," Amanda replied. She picked at the crust she'd left.

"Yeah, I know. But you said the other day you still felt you could go to him any time. Anyone would understand if you needed more sessions."

"I don't need to," Amanda snapped.

They sat in silence for the next few minutes.

"Have you looked through your mum's diary for any clues? Is it possible she could have just gone away for a bit? I know it's your dad's anniversary."

"Mum wouldn't do that. She wouldn't just up and leave like that. Somebody has got her." Amanda threw her crust into the box. "Someone has her, Poppy. I fucking *know* it."

The house phone rang, making both Poppy and Amanda jump. Locking eyes for a second, they both had the same thought. Amanda rushed over to the phone.

"Hello? Mum?" Amanda asked.

"No, I'm sorry to disappoint you, Amanda. It's Eddie…" There was a pause. "Uncle Eddie?"

"Uncle Eddie. Hi," Amanda replied, looking over to Poppy and grimacing.

"Any news? I saw the press conference. I was a little surprised not to be asked to attend if I'm honest, but if it does the job then I'm happy."

"Nothing yet. The police have nothing to go on. Pretty shit show really. It's as if they don't care. Think she's run off or something," Amanda replied, taking a seat at the dining table.

"Because of your dad's anniversary?"

Amanda fell quiet for a moment. She raked a hand through her messy brown hair. "Maybe?"

"Well, look, this is my new number." He read out the number while Amanda wrote it on a piece of stray paper from the piles on the table. "Let me know if you hear anything, OK?"

"OK."

"Bye."

Amanda put the phone down.

"That didn't sound good?" Poppy said after Amanda had returned to the couch.

"I don't really know him very well. I hardly hear from him. He was always jealous of Mum marrying into money.

Especially after he went bankrupt. He was always on at my dad to lend him more money, then when Dad said no he lost his shit and we hardly saw him after that."

"Jeez. Families, eh?" Poppy said, blowing out her cheeks.

Chapter 3

"So, Superintendent Hargreaves, do you have any new leads? It's been over a week since Diana Walker's strange disappearance. And do you think it relates to the other disappearances, as yet unexplained, in the area?" one white-haired reporter asked, holding his Dictaphone out. The group of reporters he had pushed to the front of were now standing at the bottom of the three grey flagstone steps outside Lizard Police Station. Hargreaves had finally come outside to meet them, after ten minutes of them impatiently waiting for her.

"Since I took this role last year, it is true, there have been a string of disappearances of local residents, now including that of Mrs. Walker…"

"Does this put pressure on you to resign from your post, Superintendent Hargreaves?" a different reporter interjected, and was then met with a look of disdain from Hargreaves.

"Quite the opposite actually. It's made me more committed to my job, and this town, than ever. Unfortunately, we're a small village network and have limited resources at our disposal, not to mention scarce evidence with which to mount an investigation. So, once again I would like to directly appeal to the people of this town to come forward if they have any information at all about any of these cases. The smallest piece of information could be crucial to us."

"So you think they are all related then? These disappearances?" another, much younger, reporter asked, barely giving Hargreaves time to reply.

"I'm confident we will do everything in our power to find out what happened to all of these missing persons, including Diana Walker."

"You didn't answer my question, Superintendent Hargreaves. Superintendent Hargreaves?" the young reporter repeated, but Hargreaves was already ten feet away and striding up the police station steps, slamming the door behind her.

―――――

"Hargreaves looks double pissed off this morning," Michelle said out of the corner of her mouth to the officer sat next to her, as Hargreaves walked past them both as they sat at their desks. Moments later Hargreaves' office door slammed and through the window they saw her wrench the phone handset and punch in a number. "Reckon I should wait until later to ask her to sign my holiday form?" Michelle added.

"I'd say leave it about a month?" the officer replied.

―――――

Rachel climbed off her bike and slipped her chain around it and the black iron railing, snapping the padlock securely. Something on the wheel caught her eye. "Damn it," she huffed, noticing a small piece of flint poking out the edge of her tread. Kicking the tyre, she grabbed her backpack and headed up the steps into the station.

"Morning, boss," Michelle piped up from her temporary desk in Rachel's office. "Oooh, you cycled to work this morning? So much more disciplined than me."

Rachel didn't respond, just dropped her bike helmet onto her desk with a thud next to her mug of fresh coffee. She took a thirsty slurp. "Thanks for this, Shell, much needed."

"No problem. I bet Adam was well chuffed about Spurs winning? Although he needs to start supporting a local team too. It's five years since you both moved here now. He needs to forget those posh London teams. All prima donnas. Has he been to a good old Cornish game yet?" Michelle grinned. "Get him down to Kellaway Park this Saturday. A Helston Athletic game will really get his blood pumping."

"What? Errm, no, I don't think so. I'll ask. Anyway, let's make a start." Rachel sat down and began rifling through the pages of neighbour interviews that had begun to mount up on her desk.

Michelle's face melted into a grimace. "Oh, shit, here she comes," she whispered over to Rachel.

Hargreaves loomed large over them both. "Rachel, got a minute? *Now?*"

Rachel followed Hargreaves into her office and closed the door. Hargreaves walked behind her desk and stared out of the window.

"We got anything new on the Walker case?" she said without turning.

"We're following up leads at the moment. We've conducted a door-to-door. Nothing to go on there, just a normal woman who lived a normal life. Apart from being wealthy there was nothing that remarkable about her."

"Nothing from the tip line?"

"No ma'am."

"So, what you're saying, DI Morrison, is that we have fuck all." Hargreaves turned and stared at Rachel. She hung her broad hands on her wide hips and frowned. "Remind me as to what we've done so far? Maybe then we can see what we've missed."

"Ma'am," Rachel replied. "So, as you know, just over a week ago we discussed the three grades of missing persons:

low risk, medium risk and high risk. When Diana Walker had initially been reported missing, uniformed officers had attended to complete the report. They had carried out all the usual checks, including a cursory search of the home address, just in case Mrs. Walker was ill, injured or hiding for some reason. They had spoken to her immediate family and friends, but there had been nothing to suggest that she was physically or mentally ill or in any potential danger. They had checked with local stations—in case she had been arrested—and with all the hospitals within a designated radius of the area. After I discussed the case with DI Bradshaw, it had been graded as low risk and nothing more had been done for a couple of days. When there was still no sign of Mrs. Walker, and with her daughter insisting it was completely out of character, DI Bradshaw raised the level to medium risk."

"Yes, I remember. That's when I asked you to start running a parallel investigation to the one being conducted by the Misper Unit, to see if there was any correlation between Mrs. Walker's disappearance and the spate of others that seemed to have plagued the area lately."

"Correct. I then instigated a number of enquiries. For starters, I instructed the DIU to carry out basic 'proof of life' checks. The DIU compiled a detailed research docket on Diana Walker, checking the various police databases to establish whether she had ever featured in a crime report, an intelligence report or on a Computer Aided Despatch message. A Criminal Records Office check was also conducted to see if she had ever been convicted or cautioned for a criminal offence; she hadn't. I also had one of my DCs apply to Diana's GP for her medical records in case there were any issues that the family were unaware of, such as she had a terminal illness and was feeling suicidal. Diana's GP had been extremely cooperative, having heard about her disappearance and he had made her records readily available, not demanding the usual production order from court. I also instructed a phones trained DC from the robbery squad to contact the Force Telephone Investigation Bureau and submit subscriber checks for Diana's call data and cell site. They had tried to ping the phone but it had been turned off. The call data hadn't revealed anything out of the ordinary, so I sent officers to speak to the last people she had spoken to. Nothing useful had come out of this, as you know. So afterwards, I arranged for the registration of Diana's car to be run through the automatic number plate recognition system but there had been no movement of her car since she had been reported missing. I instructed a DC who was a trained Financial Investigator to obtain a production order from a court and access her banking records. But as you know, this got us precisely nowhere. There hadn't been any activity at all since her disappearance. I then seized Diana's laptop and had it interrogated by cyber crime techs. The complete absence of activity on her phone, bank accounts and social media had deeply concerned me. That's when I advised you to make this a high risk missing person inquiry, hence the TV and newspaper appeal, the door to door enquiries and the leaflet drop being carried out. Then there was the hours and hours of CCTV we had seized and were steadily working our way through. Not usually something I would do, but I did my share. Manpower is so depleted that it was never going to get done otherwise. My team won't let up, though, until we find Mrs. Walker."

"How's that young PC I seconded over to you from Beat Crimes getting on?" Hargreaves asked.

"PC Barlow's doing a great job on this one, ma'am. She's excellent at seeking out the smallest of leads. She's so diligent. We'll get to the bottom of this, ma'am, I can assure you."

"You'd better. I'm getting reports now that this latest disappearance is starting to affect tourism. People are reading the newspapers, Rachel. The holiday brochures saying 'once you come here once, you'll never want to go home' are beginning to sound a little bit ironic now, don't you agree? The papers are starting to link these missing persons. Some are even hinting we might have some kind of serial killer on our hands. We can't have this kind of rubbish floating about. I am under pressure, which means that *you* are under pressure. I want this sorted. Quickly. Do I make myself abundantly clear?"

The cold, merciless stare that shot across to Rachel made Hargreaves' question unmistakably rhetorical.

"Bloody hell, you've gone pale," Michelle said as Rachel returned to her desk.

"Let's sort through all the paperwork, from all the cases, and look over the investigation wall again. OK?" Rachel replied. "Hargreaves will give us longer on this if we *can* establish a link."

———

"I really should leave John." Michelle sighed as she pinned up the last of the collection of photographs. "He's so fucking boring at the moment. All he wants to do when he comes home from work is eat dinner and sit and watch the footie in his pants with a beer. Eight years I've put up with it."

"Then why do you? You're not *that* bad looking," Rachel replied with a grin.

"Cheers for that. But seriously, why do I stay?"

"He's good at DIY, isn't he? And that house will never get finished without him. At least he spends the weekend doing that. He might just be knackered after work." Rachel's grin was absent this time. She picked up the first pile of notes and began pinning them around the photos they related to.

Michelle gave her a long sideways look. "I guess."

"Is she watching, by the way?" Rachel said, avoiding looking at Hargreaves' office.

Glancing over, Michelle gave a slight nod. "The blinds are shut but I can just see a little gap. I reckon she's got her beady eyes on us."

"Well, let's make this wall look as thorough as possible. We all need a result on this one," Rachel said, pinning a map on the wall. "It seems that my hunch that these mispers are linked is getting us in hot water. I am starting to wish I'd just kept my mouth shut."

"Yes, boss," Michelle said straightening the notes and pictures. She pinned up a piece of red string between all the pieces of information that linked up, then stood back to admire her handiwork. "So, you think they *could* be related then? Walker's not just gone away for a bit?" Michelle asked.

"It's possible. But none of the mispers knew each other. They lived in the same town but all have no apparent links to each other. No one saw anything, no CCTV, nothing. It's like they were abducted by aliens in the middle of the night and vaporised." She looked at Michelle and remembered. "I know, I know. You said that the other day."

"*I* was joking. You sounded serious just then. Either way, I don't think Hargreaves will sign that one off, do you?" Michelle said, looking back over to the superintendent's office.

Chapter 4

"Oh, hello. Is that Detective Inspector Morrison? It's Amanda Walker. I'm sorry to keep calling, but I just wanted to ask how the investigation is going? It's been over a week now. I'm sick with worry."

"Hi, Miss Walker. We are pursuing a few lines of enquiries. Be assured we are doing everything we can to work out what's happened to your mum."

"My uncle, Eddie Green, has been in touch. Wanting to know how the investigation was going. I gave his name to PC Barlow the other day, and he mentioned he'd had a call from the police, but hasn't heard anything back yet." Amanda's voice quivered but remained stoic.

"We've conducted some routine enquiries, yes. All immediate friends and family have been contacted for any information they can give," Rachel replied.

"There's somebody else I think you should speak to. A mechanic my mother went to just before she disappeared. Have you spoken to him yet?"

"A mechanic?"

"Yeah, I'm sure I mentioned it...or I think I did. My head is everywhere."

Rachel creased her brow and looked over at Michelle, who

flipped through all the pages of her notebook and shook her head. "Amanda, this mechanic you mentioned just now. Is there any particular reason you feel we should speak to him?" Rachel leaned forward at her desk and picked up her pen. She wrote down the details Amanda was giving her. "I see. And when did this argument happen? OK, well, I'll send someone over to speak with him. Yes, thank you. Goodbye."

"She never mentioned him when we spoke to her, " Michelle said, leaning against her desk, her arms folded.

"Apparently Diana Walker had a bit of a row with the local mechanic over some damage to her car. When he didn't admit liability, Diana took to Facebook and gave him a scathing review and demanded he get sacked for his attitude."

Michelle's right eyebrow raised. "You think there could be something in that?"

"It's all we've got at the moment to go on. Why the fuck didn't she tell me that earlier? It would have got Hargreaves off our arses if we had a decent lead to follow up." Rachel ran her hand through her hair and took a huge swig of her coffee.

"She's going through a lot. Worry will do that to your memory. Want me to get over there, check this guy out?" Michelle offered.

"Yes, please, Michelle. Let's see what he has to say on the matter. But as far as anyone else is concerned, we're only at this point investigating a missing person. Just establish his timeline for now."

"Boss," Michelle replied, grabbing her police jacket. As she headed through the exit door, in through it came another police officer. Rachel frowned as he sidled over to her.

"Alright Rach. How's the investigation going?" DI James Cooper drawled. He was just under six feet, greasy looking and built like a garden rake. The head of proactive crime was a slimy so and so, and the only thing he was truly proactive at was finding ways of avoiding anything that didn't include sitting at his desk pushing paper around.

"Good, thanks. You looking to help? I could do with some

more boots on the ground," Rachel replied, knowing full well she was wasting her time.

"Too busy, sorry. Loads to catch up on. Missed the boxing last night, but there's a great video of it on YouTube," he said. "But you and your little teacher's pet, Barlow, crack on. Nothing I like better than watching women work." He sniggered, then sloped off back to his crisp packet-strewn desk.

"Prick," Rachel muttered under her breath.

———

"Here you go, DI Morrison, one toasted cheese bagel and a flat white. No, on the house," the middle-aged owner of the high street café said with a toothy grin, tapping away Rachel's five pound note.

"Cheers, George."

"You any closer to figuring out what's going on with all these people vanishing, especially that Diana woman?"

Rachel sighed as she peeled off the lid of her coffee and emptied two sachets of sugar into it. "Nope, not yet. What are the jungle drums saying around here?"

"That the police are shit," George replied with a straight face.

Rachel nodded. "Figures. Always the police's fault, never the people who could come forward with something that might bloody well help us." She smiled at George, thanked him for the coffee and turned to leave the shop.

"If I hear of anything I'll ring you," George called after her.

"Thanks, George."

"If you ask me there's something fishy going on with that Walker case. Something doesn't add up," George shouted after her.

"Damn right," Rachel whispered.

———

"I'm gonna be the size of a whale if you keep bringing takeaways round, Pops," Amanda moaned as she opened the front door to her friend for the second evening in a row.

"You need to eat. And your cooking's shocking," Poppy replied, pushing past her and into the hallway. "Any news?"

"Nope. I've told them everything I can remember, but they don't seem to be taking it seriously." Amanda looked down at the bag of white boxes Poppy was holding. "You know, I could always come round to yours instead sometime? I hate being in this house now. Staring at all Mum's stuff."

"Oh. Well…" Poppy floundered. "You know how Mum and Dad can be sometimes. They don't understand why we're even friends, me being such a nerd and all that." She pushed her glasses back on her nose and lowered her eyes.

"You're the best friend I've got, Pops," Amanda replied, her tone flat. She walked on ahead, Poppy following her into the large, square shaped kitchen. It was just as stylishly decorated as the living room was, with white marble countertops all around the perimeter, and a white marble topped centre island. The only exception to the stainless steel integrated appliances was the cream and white coloured toaster, kettle and top-of-the-range coffee machine. Hanging from the centre of the ceiling was a gold chandelier, identical to the one in the living room, and underneath their feet was a light grey, wide slatted, hardwood floor. Above the counter that housed the butler sink was a large bay window overlooking the perfectly pruned rosebushes which bordered the huge back garden. To the far end of the kitchen was a sturdy-looking white back door.

"What about that nice detective, Morrison? She seems like she wants to help?" Poppy said as she set about laying the boxes out in front of them on the counter. Amanda didn't reply. She just sat on a white leather-topped stool at the centre island staring at her laptop screen. "What you looking at?" Poppy asked, noticing Amanda's concentrated face crease into a frown. "Someone said something online about your mum?" She walked behind her.

Amanda shut the screen with a thud. "Nothing," she snapped. Relenting, and then apologising, she reopened her laptop. "It's just…don't laugh, but I'm thinking of trying to solve it myself. I know something bad has happened to Mum. I've just got this feeling. Somebody out there knows something. The police are doing fuck all. They're not even prioritising speaking to people I've told them could be key witnesses. I'm looking up if any dodgy arseholes have been released recently from prison. There are these websites you can go on. You know, the dark web. I have to start somewhere."

"That sounds dangerous, Mand. Are you sure about getting yourself involved like this?"

"Poppy, you find using a steak knife with your dinner dangerous."

Poppy placed a hand on her shoulder. "I think you should leave it to the police. They are trained to deal with this type of thing." She watched Amanda as she spooned out Chinese food onto two clean white plates.

Chapter 5

"Morning, boss," Michelle piped up from her desk as Rachel walked in.

"How was Diana's brother when you spoke to him on the phone?" Rachel asked as she put her bag and bike helmet on the floor by her desk.

Michelle screwed her nose up. "Bit of an arrogant sod, actually. You can tell he got the shitty end of the stick. Very jealous of his sister, so it would seem. He thinks something has happened to her too. Says it's not like her to just disappear – that she's way too organised for all that. Doesn't like anyone doing things for her, so she wouldn't just leave town for someone else to mop up after her. Something was off, though. He didn't seem all that concerned about her welfare, just how it was going to reflect on him in the papers. He wants to keep his name out of it."

"Think he's involved? What's your gut saying?"

"I think we should make him a person of interest, definitely. Once we get the timeline straightened out, we can do some more digging on him. I didn't like him, anyway."

"And the mechanic? How was he when you called him?" Rachel asked, taking a sip of her coffee.

"Very angry. Told me to do one when I told him we were very concerned about the welfare of Mrs. Walker. Slammed the phone down on me, the bastard," Michelle said as she was straightening some papers.

"Really?" Rachel's eyebrows arched.

"Yep. It was just as Amanda said. I rung straight back and spoke to his boss. Apparently, Diana *had* caused a shitstorm for the mechanic down at the garage, making a complaint against him personally for some damage done to her car when it went in for a service. Massive key scratch down one side. Diana accused him of doing it as she said she didn't notice it before. His boss had put him on a final warning for his response. He said the mechanic had left for work at a normal time on the day of the complaint, and apart from being wound up there was nothing out of the ordinary to report. Although the boss did let one thing slip," Michelle said, a glint in her eye.

"Go on."

"The mechanic has a record. Did eighteen months for assault. He's out on license at the moment. One more slip-up and he's back inside. Then Diana Walker goes and makes her complaint and, well, that would be a motive for revenge, maybe?"

"It's the best lead we've got. I'll pay him a visit, I think. But first, I'm gonna call the delightful Eddie Green. Get some more intel on him." Rachel picked up the phone and dialled the number Michelle passed to her. "Hello, is that Mr. Eddie Green? My name is Detective Inspector Rachel Morrison. I'm investigating the disappearance of your—."

Rachel paused, her eyes wide as she pulled the phone away from her ear, then put it back after he'd finished his tirade.

"I understand your frustration, Mr. Green, but I can assure you we are doing everything we can to figure out what's happened to your sister. At the moment, we're struggling. There's been no phone calls made from her mobile, no texts, no use on any of her bank cards. Can you think of anywhere she might go, or any reason why she wouldn't want to be contacted?" There was a pause, the shouting on the line now hushed. "I see. When you say she didn't seem herself when you spoke to her the other week, what do you mean? OK, well, thank you for that, Mr. Green. I'll be in touch. Goodbye."

"Least I know his attitude problem towards me wasn't personal," Michelle remarked.

"He's just concerned. I'd be more suspicious if he wasn't."

Rachel's mobile vibrated on the desk. Glancing down at it, Rachel flicked it to silent.

"That your mum again?" Michelle asked.

"What makes you ask?"

"She rang while you were out. Twice," Michelle replied, sucking on a mint.

"Oh. I'll ring her later."

"Everything going OK with you two now? I remember you saying a while back you'd had a bit of a fall out? We wear a different uniform at work, but I'm your mate, remember. You can talk to me."

Rachel smiled at Michelle. She was right. Michelle had been the first PC that greeted her on her first day in the job. They'd been firm friends ever since, sharing different snippets of their very different days whilst down at the Crown for after work drinks. Her row with her mother wasn't something Rachel had told anyone about, but the day after it had happened, Michelle had noticed a change in Rachel's demeanour and had asked what was wrong.

Rachel stared down at the phone as the voicemail icon flashed. "Yeah. Mum just wants to help me talk about what happened. With Adam. And the——." Rachel swallowed and looked away so that the passing group of PCs didn't see the tear in her eye.

"You OK, Rach?" Michelle asked in a quiet voice.

"Yeah, course," Rachel replied. She dropped her phone in her jacket pocket and felt it vibrate again. "We'll talk later, OK? I'd better go and speak to our friendly local mechanic."

"Ma'am, there's a man on line 1, says he's the local MP?"

Superintendent Hargreaves sighed and flicked a hand to dismiss the young PC who'd interrupted her morning coffee. Picking up her office phone, she punched in the button. "Hargreaves speaking."

"Ah, yes. Superintendent Hargreaves, finally we get a chance to speak. My name is John Stretton, MP for Kynance Cove South. One of my constituents, Diana Walker, has been missing for a good week now and as yet there's no clear picture of what kind of investigation you are leading. Now, I can't speak for the other missing persons, I'm sure they all had families too, but Mrs. Walker is from my neck of the woods, and is quite well-known as a fine, upstanding member of the community. The press conference last week alluded to her being a missing person, and I know you have a detective inspector on the case?"

"Mr. Stretton, I can assure you I have my best officer on the case. We don't want to worry the public, which is why we aren't making too much of a fuss. We're just conducting routine enquiries and going by the book on it. We are aiming to get to the bottom of what has been going on in this town. But, as I'm sure you'll appreciate, we are severely depleted in numbers here. Recent government cuts haven't helped the situation," Hargreaves said. "If I was to be given a bigger budget, I could deploy more officers onto this case…"

There was a pause on the line before Stretton replied. "We have all been affected by the cuts, Superintendent. If I may respectfully request you keep me informed of the progress of this investigation, then I can keep the rest of my constituents abreast of what's happening also. As I'm sure *you* can appreciate, people don't know if they are living among some kind of serial kidnapper, or, well, they don't know what to think."

"You can assure your constituents, Mr. Stretton, that we are doing all we can. Good day."

Hargreaves put the phone down as gently as her rapidly growing temper would allow her to. "Fuck's sake," she muttered to herself, just as another knock rattled the blinds on her door. "What?" she barked.

"Sorry, ma'am," PC Barlow said as she opened the door a crack.

"Well, come in then, don't loiter." Hargreaves waved her hand.

"Just to keep you updated, we had a call earlier from a customer who witnessed the altercation between Diana Walker and the mechanic in town. Says it was on the day Mrs. Walker went missing."

"Where's DI Morrison?" Hargreaves replied.

"On her way to speak to the mechanic now."

"Good. Tell her to report back to me when she gets in."

"Detective Inspector Rachel Morrison. I'd like to speak with Toby Anderson, please?" Rachel announced to the floppy-haired teenage mechanic who was changing a tyre on the forecourt of the town's local garage.

"Out the back. Through there," he said, pointing towards the open gate to the side of the garage.

"Thanks," Rachel replied, putting her warrant card back in her jacket pocket. "And you are?"

"Nathan," the boy replied, wiping his nose on the back of his oily hand.

"Well, Nathan. Could you go into the office and ask the boss to come out? I need to speak with him after, OK?"

"OK." Nathan got up and walked over to the main office.

"Dad? Copper wants a word," he said, his voice trailing off into the stiff Cornish breeze.

Pushing past the long tendrils of the overgrown ferns at the side of the garage and walking through the splintery wooden gate, Rachel saw a tall young man, around twenty-five years old, wearing blue overalls splattered with grease. His messy blond hair was wiped out of his eyes by an oily hand as he turned to face her.

"Yeah? Who are you?"

Rachel took out her warrant card again. "Can we go somewhere for a little chat?"

"Look, if this is about that old bag who tried to get me the sack, then I've got nothing to say," Anderson said as he eyeballed the police badge.

"You know she's gone missing, don't you, Mr. Anderson?" Rachel said.

"Yeah. And I couldn't give a fuck," Anderson said, folding his arms.

"What exactly did she accuse you of doing?" Rachel asked, taking a step closer to him.

"She came in here just over a week ago. I serviced her car, treated her like any other customer. She drove the car away, that's it. Then the next day she came back. Said when she'd got out of the car, she'd noticed a massive scratch down one side. Started having a right pop at me, saying I'd keyed her precious BMW. Why the fuck would I do that?"

"No idea, but it's a good question. Your boss around?" Rachel asked as she looked up from making notes.

"Yeah, the cow spoke to him to get me the sack." Anderson nodded towards his boss who was on his way to Rachel, wiping his hands with a rag.

"And you will get it if you don't change your tone, Toby," came a booming voice behind them. "Bob Dixon. I own this place. Can I help you?" Dixon, a short, rounded figure in his early forties, with a shock of black hair, strode over to them and fixed his piercing blue-eyed stare on Rachel.

"Detective Inspector Rachel Morrison," Rachel replied, showing him her warrant card, then putting it back in her pocket. "I was just asking Mr. Anderson here about his altercation with Mrs. Walker. Do you remember her coming in, Mr. Dixon?"

"Of course I do. Made a right song and dance about her car. Though it didn't help when Toby here threatened to push her off that cliff over there." Dixon let out a mirthless laugh into the wind. "Said she was gonna tell you lot about him. She took to Facebook to complain about Toby. Didn't do the business too much good, I can tell ya. If you saw how many comments that kind of thing whips up." He glared at Anderson, who sucked in his cheeks.

"Well, she can't go around trying to get people the sack. How's that fair?" Anderson appealed, his hands animated.

"So you, Toby," Rachel interrupted, "made a threat and she said she was going to the police to report you. Then she goes missing. Can you see what I am getting at here?"

Anderson's face went grey. "Hang on a moment. I had nothing to do with her going missing. It was bad enough she got me suspended for two days. I got a pregnant girlfriend at home. I'm not about to go get myself in more shit now, am I?"

"Well, you've got form. Haven't you, Mr. Anderson?"

Anderson took a step closer to Rachel, who stood her ground. "Look, love, I've done my time. I paid for what I did."

Dixon put a hand across Anderson's chest. "Back off there, Tobe. The inspector's just doing her job." Facing Rachel, he smiled. "Now, was there anything else?"

Rachel looked around the yard and the side of the garage. "I'd like a copy of the CCTV footage from the day Diana Walker brought her car in, and when she came back regarding the damage. If that wouldn't be too much trouble for you, Mr. Dixon?" Rachel smiled and put her notebook away.

Anderson looked sideways at Dixon. After a moment, Dixon nodded. "No problem. I am sure he's got nothing to do with all this. I'll get it ready if you wanna pop by tomorrow?"

"That's OK, I have a pen drive here. Only take five minutes to download what I need. You've no objections, right?"

Anderson licked his dry lips and was about to speak when Dixon stepped forward and cut him off. "Sure. We've got nothing to hide. Follow me." Dixon led Rachel back towards the garage office, with Anderson trailing behind, wringing the oily rag in his clenched fist.

Chapter 6

"Oooh, nice motor. BMW 5 series if I'm not mistaken," Michelle said as she sidled up behind Rachel. The technician setting up the CCTV footage turned around in his seat and gave her an impressed smile.

"Spot on," he said. "Special edition too. Some money in that family." Turning back, he looked at Rachel. "I'll play it from the beginning. Give me the nod if you want me to pause it."

"Thanks, Phil."

Sipping the coffee Michelle had handed her, Rachel watched with eagle eyes as the technician played the tape. The footage was grainy, but Diana Walker's car was clear to see. Standing by it were two figures.

"That's Anderson there, and Mrs. Walker. Damn it, you can't see the side of the car we need. Anderson's right in front of the panel the scratch is supposed to be on. Oh, hang on, he's moved." Michelle leaned closer to the monitor and pointed at the screen. "There. See?"

"Yeah. That's one big, long scratch. Exactly where it was reported to be. But there's no footage of him actually doing it. Fuck." Rachel said.

"Doesn't mean he didn't. He at least had the opportunity.

He was standing right there. The witness to the argument said he'd heard Anderson say 'you think you're better than everybody else'. That could suggest a grudge of some description?" Michelle replied.

"Yeah, possibly. But let's keep our options open. It's circumstantial, at best. Something just doesn't sit right with me. I think I'm going to watch it until the end, then I think we should pay Mr. Anderson a little visit at home, see what his take on the footage is. For all we know, he could have been one of the last people to see Diana Walker."

"Or *the* last?" Michelle suggested, raising an eyebrow.

"Let's not jump to conclusions. We'll go round, see what his attitude is like when we tell him what we've seen on film. I'll need you and another uniform to come with me. He's not exactly going to welcome me in for a cuppa."

―――――

ARRIVING at Toby Anderson's address, a tiny two-up-two-down grey Cornish stone mid-terraced house on the Lizard high street, Rachel looked between Michelle and the uniformed police officer they'd brought along for backup, then hammered on the dark blue front door.

"Alright, alright, bloody hell," a startled voice rang out from behind the door. It opened to reveal a young, heavily pregnant woman in her mid-twenties, with dull blonde hair and tired eyes. "What the—?"

"Hello. I'm Detective Inspector Rachel Morrison. Could I speak with Mr. Toby Anderson, please?" Rachel asked.

As the young woman's response crossed her face, Anderson came storming to the door, his face like thunder. "What the fuck are you doing here? This is my home. I told you earlier, I haven't done anything wrong and here you are upsetting my fiancée. She's pregnant, you know."

"Toby, what's going on? Why are the police here? You said

you would stay out of trouble," Anderson's fiancée blurted out, her own face crumbling into confused panic.

"It's OK, babe, you go see to the dinner. I'll sort this out. Go on," Anderson reassured, ushering her away down the hall. When she was out of earshot, his softened face turned back to fury as he stared at Rachel. "Now, you look here. You've got no right coming here. What is it I'm supposed to have done that's worth you freaking out my girlfriend?"

"I just wanted to ask you a few more questions. Can we come in, please? I'm sure you don't want people in the area asking why you've got three coppers on your doorstep, do you now, Mr. Anderson?"

Anderson stood back and let them pass into his hallway.

"Michelle, go and check on the fiancée. Calm her down. Ask her if she knows anything," Rachel whispered to her, before turning back to Anderson. "So, we've reviewed the CCTV, Mr. Anderson. It would appear that you *were* one of the last people to see Diana Walker. We saw the scratch, and with that along with a witness to the conversation you and Mrs. Walker had, I'd like to conduct a search of your home."

Anderson stopped pacing the floor of his cramped living room and glared at Rachel, the merest glimpse of fear in his brown eyes. "What? No. I know my rights. You need a warrant for that."

Rachel nodded. "True. But I'd rather not have to tell my super, and your boss, that you refused to cooperate. I mean, why would you not want to cooperate? So, if you'll give us permission now, then we can crack on and eliminate you from our enquiries. That *is* what you want, isn't it?" Rachel cocked her head to the hall doorway. "For the sake of your fiancée?"

Anderson clenched his teeth and stepped aside. The uniformed officer with her started filling out the section that dealt with voluntary searches in the A4 sized Premises Searched Book that was tucked under his arm. He filled in the date, location, persons present and time of search and handed it to Anderson to read through and sign.

"Thank you, Mr. Anderson," Rachel said. "We'll give you a carbonated copy at the end of the search that explains police powers and your rights and entitlements." That done, she nodded to the uniformed police officer, who reached into his jacket pocket and took out a pair of blue latex gloves. As he began searching the property, Rachel continued to question Anderson, whose eyes darted around the room in every location the officer checked.

"Can you tell me again your movements on the day Mrs. Walker went missing?" Rachel asked, her pen poised on a fresh page of her notebook.

"What? I've said all this… Fuck's sake. I finished work and came straight home. It was a Tuesday so we watched the soaps, then the missus likes to watch *MasterChef*," he added.

The uniformed police officer returned from the hallway with Michelle, who'd left Anderson's fiancée in the kitchen to do her own search. Both officers shook their heads at Rachel.

"See, I told you you wouldn't find nothing," Anderson sneered, as the uniformed officer gave him the carbonated copy of the voluntary search form. He screwed it up and stuck it in his pocket, an arrogant grin on his face. His fiancée wandered into the living room and wrapped her arms around his waist. He lifted one arm and draped it around her. "It's OK, babe, these officers were just leaving us."

"I'll show you out," Toby's fiancée said. She walked into the hallway and towards the front door.

"Thank you for your cooperation, Mr. Anderson," Rachel said. When she was by the door about to leave, and knowing she was out of sight of Anderson, she leaned into Anderson's fiancée and handed her her card. "Call me if you remember anything. Look after yourself, and that little one," Rachel added, nodding down at Anderson's fiancée's baby bump.

Anderson's fiancée pocketed it in her dressing gown just as Anderson appeared in the hallway. She shrank slightly and returned to the kitchen.

Anderson reached out to pull Rachel back from the open

doorway. "I'm sorry if I seem a bit off, detective." Rachel turned around and saw a softer look on Anderson's face. "She's bipolar, you see. The pregnancy's just fucked up her medication so she's all over the place most days. She needs me. I can't have anything else set her off, you see? Look, what I did before I've done my time for. I'm going straight now. Trying to make a go of it. For Becca and the baby. Boss says he'll support me with the probation officer I've got, but if anything goes wrong I'll be chucked back inside. I can't have that happen. That's why I've been stressed."

Rachel looked into his earnest eyes. "Mr. Anderson, if you've done nothing wrong, then you've got nothing to worry about. I am just trying to do my job. However, I do have one question."

"What's that?"

"Do you know where Diana Walker is?"

Anderson shook his head. "No. And that's God's honest truth."

―――

"Do you believe him?" Michelle asked as she put on her seatbelt.

"Actually I do," Rachel replied starting the engine. "The fiancée corroborated his story, so you said, so there's little for us to go on." Her phone buzzed. *Where have you been?* read the message. Rachel sighed. She put her phone back in her jacket pocket, the message left unanswered.

"Well, I wouldn't put it past him, doing that. He seems a shifty bastard. Could have easily scared his missus into keeping quiet."

"Always suspicious, aren't you, Shell. But, whereas he might *seem* it, we need proof. Motive, opportunity, and all that, remember?"

"Can't we just arrest him for being a knob?"

"If only," Rachel replied, driving off. Her car phone rang.

Looking down at the display on her centre console, she groaned, then pressed the answer button. "Hello, Amanda. How are you?"

"I was just calling for an update," came the reply.

"Nothing new as yet. What about at your end? Apart from her brother, have any other of her friends or family been in contact?"

"No," Amanda replied in a quiet voice. "Have you spoken to that mechanic yet?"

"Yes, actually, we've just been to see him now. Unfortunately, there's nothing really to further investigate there."

"What? But why did he key my mum's car? Surely that alone is enough to charge him with criminal damage if nothing else?"

"The CCTV didn't show him actually committing the crime. I'm sorry, Amanda, but be assured we are doing everythin—."

"But… But what about the threat he made to Mum?"

""We've spoken to his boss, and Anderson was suspended from work. Your mother was going to file a report with the police, too. Am I right?"

"Yes. She was. This is why I wanted you to speak to him. What if he had something to do with Mum going missing? You're the police—you should be bringing him in. He could have Mum locked up somewhere. Or worse. She could be dead in a ditch somewhere. You're supposed to be helping." Amanda's voice quivered.

"We haven't got enough evidence to make anything stick at the moment, Amanda." Rachel looked across to Michelle who shook her head.

"You need to speak again with my uncle. He's due to get a lot of money if Mum ends up dead. Fuck's sake. Why am I doing your fucking job for you?" Amanda's words were now saturated with spite.

Rachel's fingers gripped the wheel tighter as she grit her

teeth. "Give me his address again and we'll go round and make some enquiries."

"Thank you."

Michelle took out her notepad and jotted down the address next to Eddie Green's phone number.

"Thank you, Amanda. I'll speak to you when we have more information." She pressed the red end call button on her console.

"Fuck's sake. First the mechanic is the perp, now the uncle? Amanda needs to back off and let us do our job."

"Would *you*? If it was your mum that was missing?" Rachel snapped back in Amanda's defence.

"Suppose not." Michelle looked out of the window as they drove back along the palm tree lined road to the station. "What does Adam think of you doing all these long hours lately?"

"He's used to it," Rachel replied, eyes focused on the road. "You're right about the mechanic, though. He did seem very worried when I told him I was taking the CCTV. It's just dawned on me now."

"Told you. He's shifty, that one."

Chapter 7

The hairs prickling on the back of her neck, Rachel couldn't shake the feeling she was being followed. She looked behind as she walked along the high street, but there was no one to be seen in the dim light of the street lamp. It was almost ten o'clock after a long day at work. Just as she lay her hand on the door handle of the off licence, her ringtone blared out.

"Shit, Mum, you made me jump," Rachel said, her free hand clamped to her chest. "Everything OK?"

"Yeah, I was just ringing to see how you are. You haven't been returning my calls. I was worried, darling."

Rachel pushed open the door of the off licence and smiled at the assistant as she began browsing. "Everything's fine, Mum. Just a case that's been taking up all my time at the moment."

"The missing woman I saw on the telly?"

"Yeah, that's the one. I just can't seem to get a hold of this one. Maybe I'm getting too stale around here. Sleepy town and all that."

"You left London for a reason, remember? You and Adam both decided a slower pace would be better for you both. A compromise, as you wouldn't give up your job. Although it sounds like you're still doing way too many long days and getting too involved again. You need to take it easy, darling. I know it's been a few years since it happened, but you don't just get over something like that straight away. It takes time. And talking about it will help."

"I know," Rachel murmured. She picked up a bottle of sauvignon blanc. "I thought it'd be different here," she said, squinting her eyes as she read the label.

"How is Adam?" her mum asked.

"We had another row," Rachel replied after a long pause. "I don't want to talk about it now, Mum."

"You know I'm always here to listen. I miss our chats. You promised me you'd keep talking to me. About your feelings. The doctor said it would help."

"I've gotta go now, Mum. I'm at the checkout," Rachel said, still standing in the aisle.

"OK, well, you just put your feet up tonight, watch a movie or something?"

"I will. *Shawshank Redemption* is on again on ITV2."

"Again? You've seen that film a million times. For a police officer, that's a very strange choice for your favourite film."

Smiling, Rachel walked over to the checkout and placed the bottle down on the counter. "Bye, Mum. We'll talk soon. I promise. Love you."

―――――

POURING a large glass of the wine she'd bought, Rachel sorted through her mail, then sank down into her armchair and kicked off her shoes. She took a gulp, then checked her phone. No texts. Calling a number, she lay her head back and took another slurp of wine as she waited for the voicemail beep.

"Adam? I'm so sorry for what happened. Sorry for everything. Please ring me back. We can talk. I just need to be able to explain. I'm sorry."

She pressed the end call button and closed her eyes as tears began to fall.

Chapter 8

"Morning, boss," the grey-haired desk sergeant said as Rachel ploughed past him. "Working on a Saturday?"

"Morning, John," Rachel replied, breathing heavily. Her face was bright red, her hair matted to her forehead with sweat.

"You on the bike again?"

"Yeah, needed to blow off some cobwebs." She smiled and waved her helmet at him as she passed.

"Blimey, judging by your face I should book you in for speeding," John called after her.

"You wouldn't dare." Rachel said, her friendly stare just sharp enough to remind him who was boss.

Upstairs, Michelle was stirring sugar into two cups of coffee as Rachel passed.

"Morning, all," Rachel said as she walked over to her office. A ripple of replies followed. "So, I was thinking we'd go over to see Amanda today," she said to Michelle as she approached holding the cups. "Give her an update, family liaison protocol and all that. We can get the inside track on this uncle of hers too. I think the more we know about this family, the better. I know we have dug into their backgrounds, but we should go over them in more detail."

"But first, essential team morale building," Michelle replied, setting down the cups on Rachel's desk, along with a packet of chocolate hobnobs.

"Morning," Poppy's cheery voice sounded as Amanda opened her front door to her and a haze of blinding sunlight.

"Bloody hell, Pops. I've never seen this much of you." Amanda sighed and rubbed the sleep out of her eyes.

"Well, I've been texting you and you haven't been returning my messages. I WhatsApped you too. I know you've read them. I saw the blue ticks." Poppy wagged her finger as she squeezed through the thin gap between Amanda and the doorframe.

"Proper little spy, aren't you? I've just been busy, that's all. I've been digging around online. You'd be surprised how much shit you can find out about people." She looked into Poppy's eyes. "Even sweet and innocent little Poppy could have a past no one knows about, hidden away on the dark web."

Poppy's eyes widened. "What?"

Amanda's stare softened into creases of laughter at the corners of her eyes. "Just kidding. Although it's worrying how relieved you look."

"Well, I just think you should leave all that detective work to DI Morrison." Poppy walked down the hallway and into the kitchen. "What are you doing today, anyway? I thought we could put another post of your mum on Facebook? You can do what's called a sponsored post, which will put it out to more people. Hopefully somebody has seen your mum by now."

"Ok, I'll try anything at this point. It's been nearly two weeks and I'm getting a really bad feeling something horrible has happened to Mum."

The doorbell chimed, making them both jump.

"I'll get it," Poppy said. She walked over to the door and pulled it open.

"Oh, good morning Miss…" Rachel began.

"Lovell. Poppy Lovell. We met briefly last week at the press conference," Poppy flicked her hair out of her eyes and pushed her glasses back onto the bridge of her nose.

"Of course we did. May we come in?"

Poppy held the door open for Rachel and Michelle to pass. When they reached the kitchen, Amanda straightened up on her centre island stool from her hunched position at her laptop.

"Do you have news?" Amanda asked.

"No, not yet. We're just making a courtesy call. See how you're holding up," Michelle replied, her keen eyes scanning the immaculately decorated kitchen, now cluttered up with takeaway boxes and used coffee cups.

"We've spoken to the locals, but to be honest we're struggling. Everyone we speak to is saying this is totally out of character, but there is no suicide note, no use of her mobile phone, her bank card hasn't been used, there's no CCTV of her catching a bus or a train, nothing. There's not even a ransom demand, so we're at a bit of a loss working out what's happened to your mother. Amanda, is there *anything* you can think of that will help us?" Rachel said, stepping closer to Amanda.

Closing her laptop, Amanda shook her head. "Only the things I've told you already."

Michelle glanced at Rachel who gave her the merest flick of her eyes. "Poppy, could you show me where the loo is? I'm bursting."

———

When they were out of earshot, Michelle stopped and turned to Poppy. "I know Amanda is probably worn out with all the stress, so I was wondering if you could think of anything at all that might help us find Mrs. Walker."

Poppy shook her head and folded her arms. "If I could think of anything, believe me, I would tell you. I can't bear seeing Amanda in this state."

"You two close?"

Poppy shook her head and blushed. "Oh, not like that. She has a boyfriend. They only got together recently, though."

"Did you know her mother well?"

"We've been friends since Amanda moved here. I think Diana liked me being friends with Amanda. Said I was a calming influence on her."

"Really? In what way?"

"Well, when Amanda lost her father, it hit her hard. When she moved here, she started having therapy to get through the grief. So her mother was grateful when I came along to be her friend."

"I see."

"Well, I'd better let you…" Poppy nodded to the bathroom door.

"Oh, right. Yes."

―――――

"So, if it's OK, Amanda, I'd like to take a look at your mother's will. It might give us some more names to investigate."

Amanda's eyes twitched at Rachel's question. "Umm…I think it's in the safe. But I don't know the combination. Mum never told me."

"Oh, right. No matter. What's the name of her solicitor? They should have a copy." Amanda fell silent. "So, how did you find out your uncle was due to get a lot of money from your mother's estate if anything happened to her?" Rachel stepped forward and leaned against the counter.

"Mum told me. A few wee…months ago." Amanda shook the fog from her brain as she tried to remember.

"Did she tell you *specifically* that your uncle would inherit?"

"Yeah. He's such a freeloader. He's never made anything of himself." The tone in Amanda's voice was impossible to ignore.

"OK, well, that gives us a good reason to want to speak with him again then." Rachel turned to leave. "Are you sure you can't remember the code to the safe?"

"It's probably your birth date," Poppy piped up from the doorway.

Both Rachel and Amanda stared back at her, their eyebrows arched.

"I mean, that's what I'd think Diana would use," Poppy said, as if a bit embarrassed for speaking out of turn.

"It's not. I've already tried that," Amanda replied. "I'll see you out."

At the front door, Rachel met with Michelle. "Thank you for your time, Amanda. We'll be in touch," Rachel said, before leaving.

Closing the door behind them, Poppy let out a sigh of relief. "Phew, that was close."

"What was? You're acting like we've got something to hide," Amanda replied, her face stony.

"I don't think what you've been researching on the internet will do you any good. The police wouldn't want you putting yourself in danger looking for shady types around this town. I'm only thinking of you. You shouldn't try and solve this yourself, Mand. If you're planning on meeting up with these people, for God knows what reason, you could get hurt. There are some nutters in this world. Let the police do their job, OK?" Poppy reached out for Amanda's wrists and stroked them with her thumbs.

"Why did you say that about the combination to Mum's safe, Poppy? Have you been poking around?" Amanda asked.

Poppy let go of Amanda's wrists and took a step back. "No. I…I didn't mean anything by it. I just figured that's what your mum would use, so she wouldn't forget. You're the most important person in her life, so I just assumed she'd use your birthday."

Amanda couldn't help but frown.

———

TAPPING her card against the contactless machine in Starbucks, Michelle looked at Rachel, who had been quiet all the way over there from Amanda's house.

"Penny for them."

"Hmm?" Rachel replied. "Oh. Just thinking about our visit just then. What do you think of the friend? Poppy. Bit too good to be true, don't you think?"

"Yeah, I thought that too. When we spoke outside the loo, she seemed like every bit the perfect friend. But you know as well as I do, nobody's perfect. I can always sense something's amiss." Michelle tapped her nose knowingly. Rachel's phone rang.

"Shit. Hargreaves," she said before pressing the answer button. "Ma'am?"

Michelle watched the expression change on Rachel's face. When the call was over, she waited for Rachel to speak.

"Fuck."

"What is it?" Michelle replied.

"Anderson has just called into the station to complain. He's in bits, apparently."

"Why?"

"His fiancée lost the baby. On the same night we visited."

"Oh, Christ," Michelle gasped.

"Shit. That poor—." Rachel's eyes looked glassy as she smacked the steering wheel with her palm, causing the car to swerve momentarily.

THE CONVERSATION back to the station was stilted, with Rachel and Michelle each feeling the stab of pain and guilt at Becca Anderson's tragic loss. Deciding to take an early finish, so as not to face the wrath of Hargreaves, Rachel asked Michelle to drop her off back at the station so she could get her bike.

"Shit!" she exclaimed, narrowly avoiding being knocked off her bike by a Mercedes. "Come on, Morrison. Get your shit together."

After locking her bike in the lean-to, she trudged up to the front door of her end-terrace house and fumbled in her bag for her keys. Her phone rang just as she poked the correct key into the hole.

"Mum, it's not a good time right now. I'll call you back, sorry."

"But you won't, though, will you? I'm worried, darling. You're not resting. You're hardly at home."

"Mum, I'm fine. I'll rest once this case is wrapped up. I promise. I've got to go."

Once inside her living room, Rachel collapsed into her armchair, the emotions of the day taking their toll on her. It was dark when she woke, her phone lighting up the living room.

"Hello?" Rachel croaked, before clearing her throat and sitting up.

"Boss, it's Michelle. I've been doing some digging on the uncle. Eddie Green? Turns out he's in shitloads of debt. He likes a bet or three. And get this, two of his businesses have recently gone tits up and he had to sell his house last year. Lives in a tiny cottage now over near Church Cove. Not only that, his wife left him and, well, I'd say that was enough of a reason to try and get hold of some money really quick, if you catch my drift?"

There was a long pause on the line. Michelle's buoyant tone dipped.

"Boss? You there?"

Rachel sniffed and wiped her face. "Yeah. Good work, Michelle. Tomorrow we can get his call data and cell site and see if his movement or contact history sheds any light on his sister's disappearance. Now go home to that boyfriend of yours. It's late."

"I know. I guess I felt so shit about what happened to Becca Anderson, I just wanted to make some headway. Maybe even take the heat off Toby?"

"I get that. But you need rest too. Go home now—that's an order. We'll go and visit Green on Monday."

"OK, boss. Night."

"Night, Michelle. And well done. Excellent work. We'll make a detective of you yet."

Rachel clicked the end call button and pressed her face back into the damp, tear-stained cushion.

Chapter 9

"Good morning, Mr. Green. I'm Detective Inspector Rachel Morrison and this is PC Michelle Barlow. Can we come in, please?"

Eddie Green, wearing a crumpled grey shirt and black faded jeans, stood at the shabby front door of his cottage looking stony faced. He ran a hand through his thick black hair. "Took your time, didn't you? I expected you last week." He stroked his unshaven chin.

"Yes, well, we've been looking at any potential leads as to the whereabouts of your sister. Shall we?" Rachel nodded in the direction of his hallway.

"Sure." He stepped back and allowed them into his home.

As Rachel scanned her eyes around the living room, with its dated beige wallpaper peeling around the damp and mouldy windows and mismatched late-nineties mahogany furniture, Michelle took out her notebook.

"So, Mr. Green, when was the last time you saw your sister?" Rachel asked.

"A few days before she went missing. I was surprised you didn't ask me to be on the press conference, to be honest," he replied, a tinge of spite in his voice.

Michelle noted this.

"We thought it would make a stronger impact if we just had Amanda there," Rachel replied. "Where were you the morning she was reported missing?"

"Lakeside Golf Club. I can't afford the green fees anymore, but they still let me drink in the lounge. There will be CCTV of me there, and the barman will remember me. I used to be a good tipper." Green half smiled.

Rachel nodded to Michelle, who wrote down Green's alibi.

"How would you describe your relationship with your sister?"

Green narrowed his eyes. "Am I a suspect?"

"We're asking everyone that question, Mr. Green. Nothing personal. So?"

After a pause, Green shrugged. "It was OK. Strained at times, but what family doesn't go through hardships?" He looked between Rachel and Michelle, his eyes softening. "She's been distant lately. Worried about Amanda."

"Worried?" Michelle said.

"Amanda's struggling still. With losing her dad all them years ago. Suicide."

"Yes, we know," Rachel replied.

"Well, after it happened, Amanda felt abandoned. She was really close to her father. Diana thought it best when they moved here to send her to a therapist, see if he could help Amanda deal with everything she was feeling."

"Are you close with Amanda?" Michelle asked.

"Close? No, not really. Never have been. Closed book, that girl." His look hardened once again. "Are we done here?"

"Almost," Rachel said. "Just a few more questions, Mr. Green, then we'll leave you to get on with your day. Did your sister ever help you out financially?"

Green recoiled ever so slightly. "What are you getting at?"

"Did she ever give you any money? Help you out?" Rachel watched his reactions carefully.

"Well, sometimes. I mean, she's my sister." He licked his dry lips.

"How much? A tenner here, a tenner there?" Rachel pressed.

Green threw his hands into the air. "Alright, alright. If you really have to know. You'll work it out eventually anyway. She sends me a direct debit every month." He looked Rachel in the face. "I'm not proud of it, you know. Needing help. But I got myself into a bit of trouble and Diana offered to help."

"How much?" Rachel asked, unmoved.

"A grand."

"Per month?" Michelle blurted out. She looked around the poky cottage, then towards Rachel, who remained concentrated fully on Eddie Green.

"Do you know anything about her will?" Rachel asked, her stare unblinking.

"Why would I? Amanda will get everything when Diana dies. Won't she?" He took a step towards Rachel. Michelle watched with keen eyes. "Look. If you think something bad has happened to my sister, then I suggest you get out there and find the person who did it. You're looking in the wrong place here. Why would I do anything to hurt the one person who's getting me out of debt right now? Think about it."

"Thank you for your time, Mr. Green. We'll see ourselves out." Rachel nodded to Michelle, who followed.

Once sat in their car, Michelle read back through her notes. "So, Amanda inherits the lot if Diana Walker turns up in a ditch somewhere?" She blew her cheeks out. "What did you make of him…the brother?"

"His reasoning sounded plausible. Get onto the solicitors, will you. See if what he says about not inheriting checks out."

"Roger that."

Rachel started the car. "There are so many holes in this case. I mean, why would Amanda be so sure her uncle was going to inherit her mother's estate? What daughter hits *that* conclusion first?"

"I know. If it was me, I'd just naturally believe it would be me if I was an only child, like her," Michelle concurred.

"When we get back to the station, you can check out the golf club alibi. That grand must be going somewhere. Perhaps he's paying off debts. It isn't going on air freshener for that shithole flat, that's for sure," Rachel said, wrinkling her nose. "Used to be a good tipper, eh?" she added, shaking her head.

"I know. I picked up on that too. But all the same, he might be a bit of a tool, but that doesn't make him a murderer. I do agree with him on one thing. Why would he do anything to his cash cow? Makes no sense. Diana Walker being around surely is to his advantage, no? She's no good to him dead."

Rachel thought about that fact for a moment, then shook her head. "Remember what he said? She *direct debits* him. So as long as there's money in there, the payment goes out automatically."

Michelle registered that fact. "Oh yeah, of course. But surely if her estate goes into probate that would be challenged by the solicitor, or whoever has the power of attorney. So he *is* a suspect then?"

"Too early to call anyone a suspect, but he's definitely a Person Of Interest. I'll take any leads at the moment."

"Possibly Amanda, too? As a POI?"

"And you know who else I want to find out more about?" Rachel added, looking on sideways at Michelle.

"Who?"

"Poppy Lovell. She seemed very quick to assume the combination to the safe, don't you think?"

Chapter 10

"Morning."

Amanda almost jumped out of her skin when she saw Poppy's cheery face peering through the kitchen bay window at her.

"Jesus Christ." She walked over to the back door and let Poppy in.

"I had a hunch you wouldn't have had breakfast. Like always," she added. "So I brought round your favourites." Poppy held up a tray of two Starbucks coffees and a brown paper bag. "Double chocolate chip."

"You not in work today?" Amanda said, taking the bag and coffees from her and setting them down on the counter.

"Start at ten." Poppy wrapped Amanda in a tight hug. After letting her go, she reached into the bag and passed her a muffin.

"Look, you don't have to keep coming round here to check on me, you know?" Amanda said, taking the muffin.

A little deflated, Poppy forced a smile. "What kind of friend would I be if I left you all on your own?"

The front doorbell rang.

"I'll get it. You drink your coffee. I got them to put a

caramel shot in it for you," Poppy said, darting off to answer the door.

Before Amanda had the chance to put in her second sachet of sugar, Rachel and Michelle appeared at the kitchen door.

"Hello, Amanda, how are you holding up?" Rachel said, her hands in her jacket pockets.

"I'm doing OK, given the circumstances. Poppy here's looking after me, as you can see." Amanda nodded down towards the coffee and muffins.

"Clearly," Michelle said.

"I'm still in my pyjamas, though, I'm sorry. Maybe if you'd called first before coming round?" Amanda pulled her dressing gown around herself.

"Oh, yes. Sorry about that. So, we spoke to your uncle."

Amanda's eyes brightened. "Did he mention the will?"

Rachel nodded. "Yes, he did. According to him, he's not a beneficiary." She watched Amanda's reactions carefully. Michelle's keen stare was trained on Poppy, who remained impassive throughout. "He stands to get nothing from the will if anything bad has happened to your mother."

"Really?" Amanda leaned back against the counter. "But why would Mum tell me otherwise?"

"That's what we've been asking ourselves too." Michelle's stare was broken as something at the kitchen window caught her attention. Seconds later there was a knock on the back door.

"Fuck's sake. Anyone else wanna pop in this morning?" Amanda exclaimed.

Rachel raised an eyebrow at her outburst. "Sorry?"

Regaining her composure, Amanda smiled. "Nothing." She looked through the kitchen window and sighed. "It's just Philippa, our resident nosey old neighbour. I can't even deal with this." Amanda rubbed her forehead.

Poppy walked over to the door and opened it. "Hi, Mrs. Beckett."

"Oh, hello, dear," Philippa said in a croaky voice as she stepped through the back door. She was in her late seventies, wearing a white knitted cardigan and a light blue blouse, with a silver brooch fastening the top two buttons together. A pair of beige trousers and brown loafers completed her outfit. Her long white hair was fixed in a tight bun on the top of her head. "I was just wondering if there was any news?" Her wrinkly grey eyes scanned each face in the room, then set upon Michelle's police uniform. "It's not bad news, is it?"

"No, we're still conducting enquiries, Mrs.?" Rachel replied.

"Beckett. Philippa Beckett. I live next door to Diana. But Amanda's probably already told you that." She smiled at Amanda. "I've been calling, dear. Leaving messages. I didn't want to bother you at this time, but I was worried about your mother. She's not returning my calls either." Philippa wrung her hands as she looked earnestly at Amanda.

"Sorry. My head's been everywhere. I would have called you if there had been any news."

"Nothing?" Mrs. Beckett replied.

"Not yet," Rachel replied, stepping forward. "I'm Detective Inspector Morrison, Mrs. Beckett." She shook Philippa's hand and gestured to the open back door. "I wonder, could we have a little chat? I'd like to ask you some questions if that would be OK?"

The elderly lady nodded and followed Rachel into the back garden. It was gorgeously appointed, with bright yellow laburnum trees bordering the far fence line, and palm trees filling the corners, providing well needed shade on that bright, sunny morning. The lawn, bordered on all sides by shrubs and flower beds, was as green as an emerald, and wafting in the air was the unmistakable scent of rosemary. Michelle stayed in the kitchen with Poppy and Amanda.

"How long have you lived next door to Mrs. Walker?"

"Oh, I was here when they first moved in over ten years ago now. I brought Diana some biscuits I'd baked as a housewarming present. Ginger they were." The old lady smiled. "Since then we've been good friends. We used to meet for coffee at least once a week. Sometimes she'd even treat us to afternoon tea."

"That's lovely." Rachel's smile hardened. "Mrs. Beckett, can you remember anything significant about the night before Diana disappeared?"

Philippa looked blank. "No. Nothing, dear. But that would be because I wasn't here. I was on my way to see my daughter in Brighton. I got back a few days ago, then found out about Diana vanishing. I have my train ticket still if you'd like to see it? I watch *Murder She Wrote* every afternoon. 2 p.m. it's on. Never miss it. So, I know how these things work."

Rachel stifled a laugh. Philippa Beckett was every bit the amateur Miss Marple. With her tight hair bun, small mouth and keen eyes, she even looked strikingly similar to Joan Hickson. Nothing more helpful when it comes to investigating a questionable family than a nosey neighbour next door, Rachel thought.

"Thank you, Mrs. Beckett. That would be very helpful to our enquiries."

"I'll go and get it now," Philippa said. She shuffled off in the direction of the side gate into her back garden.

Rachel hadn't been back in the kitchen for five minutes before Philippa's white hair bun bobbled into view through the glass in the back door.

"Here it is, inspector," she trilled, handing the train ticket to Rachel.

"Thank you." Rachel looked down at the ticket which clearly showed the date and time of Philippa's journey to Brighton. "I appreciate this."

"No problem." Philippa turned to Amanda. "Now, let me check your cupboards, dear. I'm popping to the shops this afternoon so I can get you anything you need. And have you had time to put on any washing? You've probably not even thought of that, have you?"

Amanda raked a hand through her long brown hair. "No, I haven't, to be honest. But it's fine. I haven't really got much in the basket." She rolled her eyes at Rachel, then turned back to Philippa. "But thank you, Mrs. Beckett. You're very kind."

"Well, I know your mother would do the same for my Jenny, if something had happened to me." Realising what she'd said, Philippa recoiled. "Oh, I don't mean I think something's happened to your mother. It was just a figure of speech… Oh, dear, have I upset you?"

Amanda's eyes hardly twitched. "Not at all. But if it's OK with everyone, I think I'd like to be alone now? Have some quiet time."

"Yes, of course," Rachel said, turning to walk down the hallway to the front door. "Oh, by the way, Amanda, your uncle didn't know the combination to the safe either. Looks like the contents will have to remain a mystery. For now."

Amanda smiled and waved them off as Poppy walked them to the door. Just as Rachel and Michelle were saying their goodbyes, Philippa's head popped round the kitchen doorway.

"Did I hear you mention the safe upstairs? Something about the combination?" she said.

Rachel smiled back. "Yes. But unfortunately, neither Amanda nor her uncle know the combination, so…"

"I do," Philippa replied.

Rachel and Michelle stopped and stared at her.

"You know it?" Amanda said, her mouth hanging open.

"Why yes. She told me it in case she forgot it."

"But why was she so sure *you* wouldn't forget it?" Rachel asked, walking back towards the kitchen.

"Oh, inspector. I'm hardly about to forget my own daughter's date of birth, now, am I?"

Inside the safe there was nothing seemingly out of place. The copy of Diana Walker's will sat on top of a few innocuous looking documents, the deeds to the house and some insurance paperwork.

"Just confirmed what we already thought," Michelle said with a long exhale.

"Amanda gets the lot." Rachel folded the will back up and placed it back in the safe.

———

As the group traipsed back downstairs, Poppy whispered to Amanda, "You need to tell them what you've been looking at online. These groups of people sound like not good people. I don't want you getting involved in anything dangerous. Anyway, the police might already have them on their radar."

Amanda looked at her and scowled. "I'm doing this my way. All I care about is finding Mum. And if I have to meet up with shady people to find answers, then that's what I have to do. And I don't want you blabbing to them cops, you hear?"

———

"And the prize for most helpful neighbour goes to Mrs. Philippa Beckett," Michelle joked as they walked back into the police station that afternoon.

"I know. That was a stroke of luck," Rachel concurred.

"However," said Michelle.

"What now?"

"It all seemed a little, well, err, convenient. You know. Just happening to know the number to the safe and…well…who has a ticket to hand like that?"

"Yeah, but I think she was just trying to help."

As they reached their desks, Hargreaves whipped open her door and beckoned them over.

"Shit. What now? I'm dying for a wee," Michelle complained.

"It's gonna have to wait. She looks pissed off. More so than usual." Rachel raised her eyebrows and got back up out of her seat.

They walked over to Hargreaves' office and stood in the doorway as Hargreaves returned behind her desk.

"We've had a call." She stared at Rachel and Michelle's blank faces. "From Diana Walker." She reached over her desk to the telephone and pressed the voicemail button.

"Hi. It's Diana. Walker. Look, I don't want people wasting their time looking for me. I'm not missing. I'm on a train right now. I just need to get away for a while. Have a little holiday or something? I just don't want to be found, OK?"

"Are we sure that's actually her on the phone? She was almost whispering," Michelle asked, her hands on her utility belt. "I mean, it could be any crank wanting to mess about with us." Michelle looked at Rachel, who was also confused.

"So that's that, then. No missing person to add to our long bloody caseload. Just a woman who wants the world to leave her the bloody hell alone. I sympathise. Wish people would leave me the fuck alone," Hargreaves added with a long exhale.

"Bit weird, though, don't you think, ma'am?" Michelle said to Hargreaves.

"Least she's not dead. That'll be a relief for the family," Rachel added.

"So, where does that leave us? I was quite enjoying our wild goose chase together." Michelle's voice was tinged with sadness.

"Was the call put through to you via the switchboard or is the answer phone a direct line?" Rachel asked.

Hargreaves eyed her. "A direct line. Why?"

"Because I need to get my phones man to send an urgent subscriber check off so we can confirm the number she called in from and, more importantly, find out the location of the cell that covers it."

"What?" Hargreaves spluttered. "Why? This ties things up nicely."

"And I also need to send the tape over to audio tech, ma'am. Just to rule out any chance it's a crank. I will also get Amanda to listen to it," Rachel said.

She didn't add that, at some point, she might also want a voice stress analyst to listen, in case the call was being made under duress. From her time working kidnap cases in London, she knew this happened more frequently than people thought.

Hargreaves' expression darkened. "Rachel…"

"I know, ma'am, but we need to dot the i's and cross the t's. Otherwise the papers will have a field day if it's a hoax call, right? The last thing we want is to announce that we are no longer pursuing the case and then have her turn up dead."

Throwing her arms up in the air in defeat, Hargreaves agreed. "Let me know as soon as you get a result. Then I can finally tick this one off the fuck tonne of other shit I've got to defend our force against." Hargreaves gestured for them to get out of her office. *But it doesn't explain the other missing people,* she thought.

Chapter 11

"DETECTIVE. And PC Barlow. What a surprise. What are you doing back here so soon?" Poppy said, opening the front door of Amanda's house.

"Hello, Miss. Lovell. Is Amanda home?" Rachel replied.

"Erm, no. She must have popped out. I've only just come back over myself."

Michelle eyed Poppy. "You have a key?"

Poppy swept a lock of hair from her eyes. "No. I just know where the spare is kept. I thought I'd come round and tidy up for her a bit. You saw this morning, it was a bit of a mess. Poor thing, she must really be worrying. No time for all the housework, dishes mounting up. All that. I did it before once. On her birthday. Put loads of balloons up, did the whole 'surprise' thing when she walked in. Diana wasn't too happy like. She didn't like all that fuss."

"Hmm. Do you know where she is?" Rachel asked. Poppy's eyes flashed something Rachel couldn't put her finger on at that moment.

"Amanda?" Poppy asked.

"Yes."

"I think she might have gone to the shops. I noticed there

was no milk in the fridge. I would have brought some over if I'd known…" Poppy said, looking disappointed.

"I'll call her," Michelle said, turning away from the door and taking her phone out. A few seconds later she returned, shaking her head to Rachel. "Voicemail."

Turning back to Poppy, Rachel flashed a smile. "I wonder if you could help us with something. Could we come in?"

"Sure," Poppy replied, stepping out of their way as they entered the house.

"The reason we wanted to speak with Amanda is that we have some news. About her mother."

Poppy's eyes widened. "Oh no, she's not…" She clamped a hand over her mouth.

"No, it's good news, we think. Diana has made contact." Rachel reassured.

"Really? How? I mean, when?"

"She called the station. Left a message. I just need to take a recording of her answer machine message for official comparison. Would that be OK?"

"Sure," Poppy replied, showing her to the house phone.

After Rachel had completed her recording on her phone, she turned to Poppy. "I wonder, if I played to you the recording of the call we got, could you unofficially confirm it's Diana's voice?"

"Sure. Anything to help." Poppy shrugged.

Rachel clicked on the file on her phone that held Diana Walker's message and played it loud and clear, with Poppy nodding towards the end.

"That's definitely her. I'm sure of it," Poppy confirmed. "She doesn't sound herself like, but Amanda will be made up. But… Oh no."

"What? What is it?" Rachel asked, taking a step closer.

"Oh shit. I'm not supposed to tell you. But I'm worried now." Poppy put her hand over her mouth. Rachel and Michelle stared at Poppy. "Well, Amanda was getting impatient with you lot. Not finding any leads and that. So…"

"Where is Amanda, Poppy?" Rachel demanded.

"I genuinely don't know *where* she is. She made me swear I wouldn't tell you. But she was looking online for records of dodgy people and anybody released from prison recently. Anyone in the newspapers who'd done time for kidnapping or assault. Or even murder." Poppy gulped. "She's been following them for a while to see where they go. Most of them end up in pubs on the outskirts of town, so Amanda just watches them to see where they go, in case it leads her to her mother. But now her mother's alive. Oh Christ, Amanda needs to know."

"Right, you tell her we called when she gets back, OK?" Rachel ordered before turning back to the door and leaving, closely followed by Michelle.

———

AMANDA PUSHED OPEN the door of the Anchor Pub and was immediately hit by a wall of noise. The bar was crowded with men all wearing football shirts and yelling abuse at the referee, who had clearly made a poor decision. In the far corner was a small group, having a quiet drink together. A middle-aged woman wearing a navy blue parka sat drinking an orange juice. Next to her sat a younger man wearing blue stonewashed jeans, a dark blue hooded jacket and black steel toe-capped boots. The third man at their table was a few years older than the first man. He had lighter coloured brown hair and looked as if he'd come straight from work, in his pale blue shirt and a navy and white striped tie. The two men had untouched pints in front of them. Amanda watched them for a few minutes, and in that time they said absolutely nothing to each other.

"What can I get for you, love?" a middle-aged, portly looking barman with dark curly blond greasy hair asked.

Amanda looked up at him. "Oh, I'm just waiting for someone."

The barman huffed. "Suit yourself." He walked back over to the other end of the bar, wiping his hands on a tea towel. The group of football supporters broke ranks as the half time whistle sounded, with a couple of them heading to the toilets and the others dissipating among the other patrons in the bar.

Amanda sat on a bar stool and absorbed the surroundings of the bar. That afternoon she'd read online that the Anchor was a known breeding ground of various dregs of society and, with its remote location half a mile from Lizard Point, it rarely suffered from any police intrusion. Even the hardest of officers knew better than to take on swarthy locals so close to a 200 foot cliff edge. She looked up at the TV screen now showing the news.

"Sad, isn't it? All those people going missing?" The barman from before said as he wrapped his tea towel around the rim of a glass. He nodded up to the news broadcast now showing the pictures of the missing people from the area.

"Did they come in here?" Amanda replied, not really listening to him but keeping her eyes fixed on the screen.

"No. But if you ask me, that group over there must have known them." He pointed to the group in the corner that had caught Amanda's eye when she walked in. Amanda turned to look at them.

"Why?"

The barman laughed. "Because the people who went missing were a doctor, a teacher and a businesswoman's wife. That group over there?" He leaned over the bar, close enough for Amanda to catch a whiff of his sour breath. "I got chatting to the woman one night a few weeks back. Found out she's a nurse at the same hospital as the doctor was at. The older man is a teacher—at the same school my daughter goes to—and the same school the teacher that went missing taught at."

"And the pretty boy?" Amanda asked.

"Not sure about him. Must just be friends with the bloke maybe. I thought he might be a gardener, what with all the grass he traipses in here." The barman grinned. "I watch a lot of Columbo. He'd notice stuff like that, you know? Anyway, that lot over there meet here once every month, then go off for a walk somewhere. Bit suspicious if you ask me."

"Hmmm," Amanda remarked. "I'll have a rum and coke," she said, smiling at the barman, who obliged. As she took a sip, Amanda watched the group more closely. When they drained their drinks and got up, she did the same. Trying not to be noticed, she slipped out of the pub twenty seconds after they did.

THE WIND UP on the cliffs of Lizard Point was stronger than usual that evening. Amanda didn't care. Leaving her car at the Anchor Pub car park, she had walked in the twilight, along the southwest coastal path, with the group from the pub just far enough in front for them not to notice her following them. About half a mile ahead, overlooking Hounsel Bay, was a rugged looking whitewashed stone lighthouse, dominating the landscape in front of her. The shrubs she'd stopped to hide behind provided just enough cover for her to watch and wait to see what the group did next. No one had lived in the lighthouse for fifty years or more, the only official key holder being a local fisherman who acted as the custodian.

But now it would seem there was at least one *unofficial* key holder.

Amanda watched with keen eyes as a figure wearing a dark hoodie pulled tight around their face, black jeans and heavy looking boots approached the door of the lighthouse where the three people from the pub were waiting. They all looked around cautiously before the first figure pulled out a key and they all disappeared inside.

"What's going on in there?" Amanda muttered to herself as she watched.

"Morrison," Rachel said after pressing the answer button on her hands free.

"Boss, it's Andy. I've finished running that tape."

"And?" Rachel snapped.

"Well, we've isolated all the frequencies away from the vocals, and picked up a few strange sounds in the background."

"Get there quicker, Andy."

"Well, the weird thing is, she says she's on a train, right? Well, we heard on the track what sounds like the tune a washing machine plays at the end of its cycle in the background. It's only faint, though, but we have made it out."

"What? One of those annoying fucking singing ones?"

"Yep. Very common these days. But each brand plays a different tune, so I'd go speak to a few retailers, maybe a specialist in this field. I'm emailing you the enhanced audio track now."

"Thanks, Andy, you're a star." Rachel hit the end call button.

"A washing machine tune in a train carriage?" Michelle asked, looking at her in bewilderment in the passenger seat. "What the fuck is going on?"

"As if this case wasn't weird enough. Now we've got to go to every pissing Currys in Cornwall and play Name That Tune to every washing machine geek we can find." She reminded herself to chase up her phones' technician. Identifying the telephone mast that covered the location where Diana had called in from suddenly seemed very important.

———

"Amanda, where are you? That detective, Morrison, has just been here. She has an audio of your mum calling the station. It definitely sounded like her, so that's good news, right? Your mum said she didn't want to be found, but at least she's safe. Please come home, Amanda. Don't go looking for psychos.

I'm worried you're getting in over your head. You don't need to do that now. Just come home, OK?" Poppy sighed and put down the phone. "Call me back when you get this message. Just let me know you're alright. Please? I'm worried about you. Bye."

———

THE WAVES below crashed mercilessly against the jagged bastite rocks of Lizard Point, with the glimmer of moonlight catching in the greeny-brown flecks of serpentine. Stepping through the long grass, mindful to watch her every step as she was so close to the cliff edge, Amanda crept up to the lighthouse and flattened her back against the whitewashed Cornish stone. She slid her body around the curved wall and pushed on the entrance door. To her surprise it creaked open.

"Didn't expect that," she whispered to herself.

Inside it was almost pitch black. Amanda lay her palm against the damp bricks and felt her way along, her eyes already adjusted to the dark after her walk over from the pub. The room she appeared to be in was cold and smelled musty, with just a tinge of saltiness from the sea air outside. Up ahead, she could just about see the outline of a flight of concrete steps with a metal railing guiding the way upward into nothingness. Just next to it was a wrought iron spiral staircase. The light just visible at the bottom of it was the deciding factor to Amanda. She walked over to the staircase and began to descend it, one careful step after the other, her trembling right hand gripping the handrail. At the bottom there were three doorways, each with a sturdy wooden door blocking her path. As Amanda stepped over to the door on the right of her, the door on the left swung open. In the torchlight that was now almost blinding her, Amanda stumbled backwards, her forearm clamped over her stinging eyes.

"Who are you?" a sharp female voice sounded. She continued to shine the torch in Amanda's face.

"Ermm... I'm Amanda. Who are you?" Amanda grimaced as she strained her eyes through the crack between her arm and face.

"What are you doing here? You can't be in here." The short and stout woman's blue eyes were wide as she darted her gaze from side-to-side, then up at the staircase Amanda had descended. "You need to go. *Now*. Before the others see you."

"What the…" the tall, well built, youngish looking man from the pub with short, dark brown hair and frightened brown eyes began, before glaring between the woman and Amanda. "Who's this?"

"Says her name is Amanda. But I wasn't told there would be another joining us tonight," the middle-aged, lighter-haired woman replied.

"Me neither." The young man's face hardened with suspicion.

"Joining?' Amanda asked. "Look, I'm not sure why I've come—."

She took Amanda by the hand. "Come with us."

"Where to?" Amanda replied, allowing herself to be walked into the room the man had come out of.

"To meet the other one," the woman replied.

The next room Amanda found herself in was a little lighter, illuminated by a lone lightbulb dangling down from a solid looking wooden beam. A large heavy table dominated the room, with four chairs tucked neatly underneath. In the corner, on a trestle table, was an oblong tray of teacups and a kettle. Next to it was a small box of teabags, a pint of semi-skimmed milk and a packet of digestive biscuits. Whatever was due to be happening in this room tonight clearly hadn't started yet. Out of one dark corner of the room another figure emerged.

"No one told me we were having a new person tonight," the man from the pub wearing the shirt and tie said. Taking out a packet of cigarettes, he lit one, then blew out a cloud of smoke and coughed.

"None of us were told," the woman replied, her tone short. "Put that fag out. You've been told about doing *that*," she snapped, wafting away the smoke.

"Fuck's sake." The man dropped his cigarette to the stone floor and crushed it under his brown loafer. "Look, no offence, love, but how do we know you ain't gonna talk, huh?"

He walked over to Amanda and eyeballed her.

Amanda shook her head. "I wouldn't. Why would I?" she said, her voice even.

"You know The Therapist?" the first man piped up from the doorway.

Amanda nodded. "Yeah. We go way back. They told me to come tonight. Said you'd all be here."

The air around them all seemed to grow cooler, stiller, by the second. The three strangers looked at each other, trying to read each other's thoughts, until the middle-aged woman shrugged.

"OK, I'm sure you wouldn't be here, on this same evening, for any other reason than what we're here for," she said, wandering over to the tea tray.

"What do you do down here…exactly?" Amanda asked. She took a step forward, and into the full glare of the light-bulb above.

"Hey, hang on a minute," the second man said. He pointed two shaky, cigarette-stained fingers at Amanda, his eyes staring. "You're that girl off the telly. The one whose mum's missing."

Amanda's stomach lurched. She nodded. The room fell quiet. The woman put down her teaspoon and stared at Amanda. For the whole three minutes of the kettle boiling, nobody uttered a word.

"Did you…do the same as we did?" the first man said, his voice barely above a whisper.

"Do what?" Amanda asked. Her palms felt moist, her mouth dry.

"Make someone disappear," the woman answered.

Poppy pressed the end call button on her mobile after leaving yet another message for Amanda and threw it onto her bed. She paced the floor of her bedroom and sank down, wrapping her duvet around her. Checking the time on her phone seconds later, she let out a long exhale.

"Where are you, Mand?" she said into the air, her tired eyes closing.

In the darkness, the phone lit up, making Poppy jump. Fumbling in the duvet to grab the phone, she jabbed her finger at the answer button.

"Mand?"

"Hello, Poppy? It's Detective Inspector Morrison. I was just calling to see if Amanda has turned up yet, but judging by your voice I'd say not."

Poppy ran her hand through her tousled hair and rubbed her eyes. "Hello, detective. I've not heard from Amanda yet. I'm really worried. I'm starting to think the worst."

"You think she could have harmed herself?" Rachel asked.

"Or been hurt by those psychos she's been tracking down. What if her mother *has* been abducted by them? And now Amanda has too? Oh, it's such a mess, detective. Can you help? Please?"

The tension in the air was palpable. Amanda, frozen to the spot, fought to straighten out the racing thoughts in her head. Fight or flight was kicking in.

"If you don't mind, I don't really know anyone here yet. I'm sure you understand I'm a bit reluctant to open up to strangers. I don't even know your names." She let out a mirthless laugh.

"Of course. We understand. As for our names, well, we don't go by our real names. I'm The Nurse. That there," she pointed to the first man, "is The Gardener, and," she nodded to the second man with a freshly-lit cigarette, "he's The Teacher."

The two men nodded their acknowledgement. The Teacher walked over to The Nurse and took his mug of tea from her. "I guess we could call you The Daughter, then? How's that?"

Amanda replied with a tight smile.

"So, now you know who everyone is, there's just one more thing I'd like to know," The Nurse stared at Amanda. Amanda swallowed. The Nurse's hard face melted into a warm smile. "Sugar?"

"Yes. Two. Thanks," she replied.

"Relax. I don't think any of us will be calling the police on you anytime soon, so your secrets are safe with us," The Teacher said, seating himself at the table as another mug was put in front of him by The Nurse.

"If we did, we'd *all* be gonners. One goes down, we all go down," she said, offering everyone a digestive.

Amanda waved hers away and sat at the table opposite The Teacher. "Really?"

"You bet, after what we've done. That's why we're here. To talk about it with people who understand. How else are we supposed to live with it? It was The Therapist's idea. Think of it as kind of like an AA group," The Nurse said, trying to get comfy on her wooden chair.

Another long pause hung in the air as The Gardener sat down at the table. The four of them sat equidistant from each other, as if they were about to begin a séance.

"So, did you do it?" The Teacher asked while dunking his biscuit.

Amanda looked at The Teacher, who slurped his tea. "Do what?"

"Have her removed. Your mother."

Amanda played along. "Why? What do you know about it?" She lay her palms flat on the table and stared back at him.

"Calm down, dear. Here, have a biscuit." The Nurse held out the packet again, her hand visibly trembling, her face pale. "We're all here for the same thing. Nothing we can do about it now. We have to live with what we've done." She nibbled on the edge of a biscuit.

"We're here to help each other cope with what we've done," The Teacher said. Looking at Amanda, he smiled. "That's why he asked you to come too. Isn't it?"

"Who?" Amanda asked.

"The Therapist. He helps us all come to terms with our guilt."

"I don't know what to say. My head is such a mess." Amanda ruffled her hair and refocused her eyes on the group. "I'm sure you understand that, right?" The three nodded. "So, what happened with you?" Amanda said to The Nurse.

"Me? Well, I didn't have any choice, really. I did what I had to do." She took a sip of her tea as Amanda waited for her to continue. The men, having heard the story before, looked down at the table, each drifting off into their own worlds. "Back where I used to work, at West Cornwall hospital over in Penzance. You know it?"

Amanda nodded.

"Well, there was a doctor who'd just started working there. A right Flash Harry he was. Thought all the girls wanted to go out with him. Total bastard, I thought. Anyway, he was everyone's favourite doctor. But one day I found out he was sexually abusing a patient. She told me just before she died, in *very* suspicious circumstances. So, I put in a complaint. I was convinced he'd finished her off so I reported it to the police too, but nothing was done. There was no investigation. Nothing. Everybody loved him. He had them wrapped around his little finger. I went to that poor girl's funeral, even though by that point I'd been suspended from work, and he came over to me. Admitted what he'd done to her. Whispered in my ear, the bastard. I was livid, but he hugged me so from a distance it looked like, yet again, he was being the bigger person. After that, there was no way the complaints would be upheld." She paused for another sip of her tea.

"Why?" Amanda asked, leaning forward in her chair.

"Because all the patients I knew he was abusing mysteriously passed away whilst in hospital. Never recovered from what they were brought in for." She snorted. "Some only came in with minor illnesses. Nothing life threatening. But for each one it was put down to foreign nursing staff 'missing' things. So these poor nurses were 'moved on', let's say. People die every day in hospitals. Sometimes it's unavoidable, but sometimes it's a mistake from some junior doctor or nurse. Nothing malicious, just a cock-up brought on by long hours and overstressed staff. So, when it happens the hospital keep things quiet and everyone turns a blind eye. No one ever suspected their blue-eyed, perfect doctor. No one to validate what I knew he was doing, time and time again. Well, I just couldn't let another innocent person die at his hands. That was the last straw, when poor Ruby died. I promised I'd take extra care of her, after what she told me that bastard was doing to her. She was only sixteen, bless her. Only had foster carers to speak of, no one really that gave a shit. So, she didn't have any visitors. I think that's why he chose her for his next victim."

As The Nurse was about to begin her next sentence, Amanda's phone blared out its ringtone, making all around the table jump.

"Fuck's sake. Sorry," Amanda said, fumbling in her pocket to kill the phone. "Sorry, go on," she said, fiddling with the phone, saying that she was putting it on silent, then back in her jacket pocket.

"So that's when I knew I had to do something," The Nurse said, taking a sip of tea. "To stop the next poor girl he came into contact with getting hurt. Or boy. He told me that day at Ruby's funeral he had a new interest in his sights. I think he liked the power that he had over me, that I knew about what he was doing and couldn't stop him. It was a game to him."

Amanda remained emotionless.

"I was sick of reporting it. For what? To be seen as *that* crazy middle-aged woman who's looking to trash a young, dynamic doctor? No thanks. No, he had to go." She sipped her tea again, at length this time.

"You did the right thing. One less sick fuck on the planet is best for everyone," The Gardener said, folding his arms.

"What was his name?" Amanda asked.

"Jerry Carter…the bastard."

Amanda sat up straight. "I know that name. I saw it on the news. He's one of the missing, presumed dead people in this town." Her mind was racing. She suddenly became very aware of the confined, and secluded, space she was currently sitting in.

"Good riddance, that's what I say," The Nurse said, smacking her lips. "Well, that's my story."

"So how did you do it? How did you get rid of him?" Amanda asked.

"Well, that's one part of the story I can't take credit for."

―――

It was almost 10 p.m. when Rachel's phone illuminated her living room. Lifting her head from her couch cushion, she fumbled under the throw. "Morrison."

"It's Hargreaves. Just calling for an update on the audio. Did you confirm it was Diana Walker?"

Rachel sat up and rubbed her eyes. "Ma'am. So, it's a bit of a weird one, really."

"In what way?"

"Well, yes, we had it confirmed that it is Diana's voice on the message. But just when we thought she's turned up alive, but just not wanting to be found…it seems that message she sent has some strange anomalies on the enhanced audio track.

Not only that, but…" Rachel paused to clear her throat, to the annoyance of the ever-impatient Superintendent Hargreaves.

"Spit it out, inspector."

"Now Amanda's gone missing."

"For fuck's sake. When?"

"Her friend Poppy hasn't seen her all afternoon or evening and can't get in touch with her. Her phone's just going to voicemail."

"She's probably just wanting some space. What makes you so sure she's gone missing?"

"Well, Poppy let slip that Amanda's been investigating her mother's disappearance herself. She's been looking up the names of criminals in the local area in the last few weeks. We haven't even been able to get in touch with her yet to tell her that her mother is alive and well. She could have put herself in danger, for no reason now."

"So who confirmed the audio if Amanda wasn't there?"

"Poppy," Rachel replied. "She knew Diana well. Amanda and she have been friends for years. She's really worried about Amanda not coming home."

"Great," Hargreaves replied. "I can't *wait* to tell the press this little nugget of shittery. What are the anomalies?"

Rachel filled her in.

"So, are you thinking this message from Diana could be fake, then?"

"I'm not sure at this point. The subscriber check confirmed that the call was made from Diana's telephone number but then the system crashed and the service provider won't be able to provide the cell location until they're back up and running. Until I get the cell site data and can establish whether the tune they picked up in the background was coming from a washing machine, and not some weird train announcement, I'll be none the wiser. The only consolation is that Poppy confirmed it's definitely Diana's voice, so that's half the battle."

"Wait a minute." Something dawned on Hargreaves. "So,

the only confirmation Diana Walker is alive is from the clingy best friend who keeps letting herself into Amanda's house, and by all reports from PC Barlow is a little bit too perfect?"

"There is something about Poppy I can't quite put my finger on, yes. But at the moment there's no motive for her to have done anything. She just really cares about her friend. It borders on love, if you ask me. But to be honest right now, I'm just piecing all the fragments together." Rachel rubbed her temple. "There's one more thing."

"Go on."

"Well, it seems a bit strange to me that Diana Walker decided to phone us and not her daughter. What do you think?"

"Yeah, that is a bit strange. But it might be that Mrs. Walker didn't want to speak to her. People do strange things all the time."

Rachel paused. "It was just a thought."

"Look, I don't know where your head's at right now, Rachel. But from where I'm standing it doesn't sound like Diana Walker has taken some train to sanctuary. We've had the CCTV from all local train stations looked at. No sign of her. Also, what did she use to pay for her ticket, Scotch mist? We might not have a motive, but that Lovell girl had the means and opportunity to get into the house with the spare key, so that's why there was no forced entry present. Also, Walker knew her, so trusted her. I want that girl brought in and questioned. We need to box off this case, quick smart. We need to find Diana Walker, or the press will have a field day. Do I make myself clear?"

"Yes, ma'am. I'll speak to Poppy tomorrow."

―――

THE LIGHTBULB above the table swayed as another gust of wind buffeted against the lighthouse. The waves in the distance continued to lash the rocks.

"So, what happened?" Amanda asked The Nurse.

"Well, I was so torn up by not being believed at the hospital that my husband paid for some private therapy, due to the stress of it all. He could see how much it was getting me down, working with this monster. I'd already been suspended for the allegations, but now they were talking about making it permanent if I kept this 'vendetta', they called it, up. Almost thirty years as a nurse, all for nothing. No job, no pension."

"That's shit," Amanda said.

"So in my therapy sessions each week, I talked about it. And the therapist listened. And listened. Until one day he finally said, 'What would you say if I told you I could get rid of the problem for you?'"

"Meaning the pervert doctor, right?" Amanda asked.

"Yes. I thought it was a joke at first. A test to see what I would say. Maybe testing my mental state, perhaps? But I wasn't crazy. I was angry at the doctor. Working with that predator day in, day out, you should hear what he said to me. I was putting up with it so I could try and protect as many vulnerable patients as I could. Well, I couldn't face doing that forever. What if I got sick and couldn't go in one day? How could I live with that being the day someone else died? When the therapist alluded to another type of justice, well, what can I say? It sounded appealing."

"What did he say?"

"He asked me to give him details of the doctor's whereabouts, his movements, where he hangs out after work, all that kind of thing. I managed to get his address. And one of the last things the therapist asked was, 'Are you sure you want this to go ahead?'"

The Teacher and The Gardener looked at each other, then at Amanda. The Gardener watched her reactions especially keenly.

"So then what happened?" Amanda asked.

"I nodded. The Therapist told me to ask no questions, not act any different and he said he would now take care of it. I wouldn't know when. There are a few people involved, but we all don't know each other. Safer that way, I guess. Then we all can't tell on each other. And as expected, four days later, the bastard didn't show up to work. The hospital reported him missing, and all kinds of things got said, like he'd topped himself, gone off with somebody else. But I knew what had happened. I had my normal weekly therapy session and I was just told it was 'sorted'. Now as much as I'm happy about that, that no doubt he is buried somewhere, I have to live with that." She paused and began fiddling with her wedding ring. "This kind of thing isn't me. I've lied to my husband, my daughter, my colleagues… I'm responsible for somebody's murder."

"Sounds to me like the bastard deserved it," Amanda said. "I bet he squirmed while they were finishing him off."

"He did deserve it. I know it was the right thing to do, for all those patients he won't have the chance to hurt. But it was on my conscience and that's what this group is for. The Therapist knows that we all can't just live with this, so he created this little group. It gives us a chance to get things off our chest and makes it less likely one of us will crack and start talking to a stranger. Clever when you think about it. For the three of us, and now you, who have to live with being responsible for ending people's lives. We may not pull the trigger, but we are just as guilty."

Amanda swallowed and licked her dry lips. "Where is he buried?"

"Oh, we never get told that... Ever… It's so we can't get interrogated. We don't know anything. Only The Therapist knows."

Amanda looked at the two men across the table. "What's your story?" she said to The Teacher.

He remained quiet for a few moments. After fiddling with his tie knot, loosening it slightly, he shuffled in his chair and folded his arms. "I was also having stress therapy. There was this guy teaching at the same school as me. I'd noticed him acting inappropriately towards some year elevens he was teaching. Same as The Nurse really, I spoke up, but no one believed me. No hard evidence, and none of the girls wanted to make a complaint. Why would they? They didn't understand what he was doing. They got A grades, lots of attention, and loads of school trips. Even though half of the trips were nothing to do with the subjects he was teaching. The school saw it as enrichment of the curriculum, so they were happy. But the things I saw were disgusting." He paused to take a long drag on his cigarette.

"One day, after school, I went back to a classroom I'd done a cover lesson in, as I'd forgotten my laptop. I heard a noise in the stockroom at the back of the classroom, so I peeked through the crack in the door. He was in there with his hand down the front of a year eleven girl's blouse. She was looking up at him through doe eyes as she was wanking him off. He saw me and threw me against the wall. Told me if I said anything he'd rape my niece who went to the school. The year eleven girl just laughed at me and said she'd deny it if I told anyone. I think she was in love with him. Anyway, the next morning I saw a poster on his classroom door. He was planning to take his year eleven geography class on a field trip to New York. But my niece was also in that class and there was no way I was letting him near her. I wanted her out of his class, but she assured me nothing was happening to her. But I couldn't take the risk that something *might* if she went on this trip. Her mother didn't believe me, and because I'd made such a racket about my concerns the head wouldn't even allow me to go on the trip to keep eyes on that teacher. He said it would cause 'unrest between the others'. Can you believe that?"

"So what did you do?" Amanda asked.

"I told The Therapist, who responded in the same way he did to The Nurse. Asked me if I wanted something to be 'done'. Of course I did. What choice was there? Anyway, the teacher disappeared and the trip never went ahead. He's still registered missing. But he won't be coming back."

"I remember. There was a teacher in the list of missing persons I saw on the news. Ryan something." Amanda nodded.

"There you are then."

All eyes fell on The Gardener.

"So, what's your story?" Amanda looked at him. He looked down to his steel toe-capped boots and fiddled with the edge of the table. Before he could answer, The Nurse looked at her watch.

"My *goodness*, is that the time? We've been here for nearly two hours. My husband's going to be calling the police to search for *me* if I'm not back soon." She looked at Amanda. "Listen, we normally meet once a month to talk things over. Why don't we all come back tomorrow night? You haven't had the chance to talk about why you're here."

"I can do tomorrow night. The wife is at her book club so she'll be out until late," The Teacher said.

All three pairs of eyes fixed on The Gardener.

"I'm not sure. I might have to be in tomorrow night. It's not good for me to be out two nights in a row."

"I'm sure it'd be OK. I can ask a friend of mine to go check on Jamie while you're out," The Nurse said.

"I guess."

"That's settled then. Amanda, sorry, Daughter, can you make it?"

Amanda smiled. "Sure. Same time?"

"Eight thirty p.m. sharp," The Teacher said. "I'll walk you to your car."

AMANDA and The Teacher walked along the coastal path back to the pub where their cars were parked. Once they were out of earshot, The Gardener pulled back The Nurse's arm as she was locking the front door to the lighthouse.

"I can't do this. What is he playing at bringing another

person into our group? I thought it was just us." He bit down on a fingernail.

"She's in the same boat as us. Give her a break. And anyway, now we've got another member of the group, maybe she can get you to open up more. We've been coming here for almost six months now, and both me and The Teacher have noticed you've not been the same this last week or so. Maybe tomorrow you can get whatever it is that's bothering you so much off your chest?"

"I can't. No way. I won't be here. I can't do this anymore."

"You have to. The Therapist said we should attend all sessions."

The Gardener ran a shaking hand through his dark brown hair and left her by the door.

———

AMANDA SAT in her car and locked the doors. Fishing her phone out of her pocket, she saw on the display there were fourteen missed calls from Poppy, and five voicemails. Playing the first one, she growled. "Hi Amanda, it's Poppy. I was just ringing to see if you were OK? Call me when you can. Bye." Then the next one. "Amanda? It's Poppy again. I was thinking I could bring round a pizza? OK, speak to you soon." Then the third one. "Hi Amanda, I've just got to yours and I hope you don't mind but I let myself in. I'm worried about you. Where are you? OK, call me back when you get this." Then the fourth one. "Amanda, it's Poppy. The police have just been round again. They want to talk to you. Your mo—."

Amanda hit the end call button.

"Fuck's sake, Poppy, leave me alone for five minutes, won't you?"

As she was about to start the car, her phone rang again. This time it was her uncle's number that flashed up on the display. "Hello?"

"Amanda, thank God. Where the hell have you been?

Your crazy mate's been ringing me all evening. Said she's staying at your place until you come home." Eddie Green's gruff voice pounded Amanda's eardrums.

"Look, I just needed space. I'm not coming home tonight. I'm going to get a hotel."

"OK, but keep your bloody phone on, will ya. I'm sick of having people bugging me all the time looking for you."

"Bye."

Amanda hit the end call button, then switched her phone off before throwing it onto the passenger seat. Noticing a sign above the Anchor Pub doorway saying they had rooms to rent, she climbed out of the car.

Chapter 12

"Afternoon, boss. How was your evening?" Michelle asked as she got into Rachel's car.

"Shit. I was knackered," Rachel replied.

"I was a bit worried about you. After we found out about Becca Anderson and the baby, you seemed... I texted you when I got home, but…"

"I'm fine. Sorry I didn't text back. I fell asleep on the couch. I was going to take the morning off, you know? Recharge the batteries. But then Hargreaves rings me, wanting me to go and bring Poppy Lovell in for questioning."

"About time, if you ask me. Well dodgy, that one."

As they rounded the next corner, Rachel's car phone rang. "Morrison."

"Detective, it's Becca Anderson."

Rachel and Michelle looked at each other.

"Hi Becca, how are you feeling? I was so sorry to hear—," Rachel said in a voice so soft it surprised Michelle.

"Listen, I need to speak with you. It's urgent. There's something I didn't tell you. About that night Diana Walker went missing? Toby *did* come home late. I'm so sorry I didn't say anything before. I just wanted to protect him. He didn't come straight home from work like he told you. He didn't come home until late, and then when he came in, he got changed and put his clothes straight in the washing machine."

Rachel shot a glance at Michelle, whose eyes widened.

"I was surprised he even knew how to switch it on. He's never done a load of washing in the whole time I've known him."

"Becca, would you be able to point out the clothes he was wearing that night for us?" Rachel asked, knowing that, with the advances in modern science, it was still often possible to detect microscopic traces of DNA on clothing, even after it had been put through a stringent wash cycle.

"Yes, I know exactly what he was wearing and where it is now," she said.

"OK, Becca, thank you. That's really helpful. I'll be in touch." Rachel punched the end call button on her steering wheel and took the next exit off the roundabout.

"Well, well, well, our friend Anderson may be a lying little toe rag after all," Michelle said. "Washing machine too, eh? Straight round there?"

"Oh yes. It's time Toby Anderson told us the truth about Diana Walker's disappearance. Michelle, phone the office. Get Kev and Matt to drop whatever they're doing and meet us over there on the hurry up, just in case we need some muscle."

They sped down the high street and turned left at the lights onto the road leading to Dixon's Autos. Already there when they pulled up was an unmarked police car, its back lights flashing blue. Inside sat two solid looking men.

"What I don't understand is why Becca didn't just tell us when we were over at her house. She could have told me at least when we were talking alone in the kitchen," Michelle said, shaking her head.

"Probably couldn't handle him going back inside again. Not with a little one on the way. Well, not anymore," Rachel added. "Probably thought, 'Fuck it, I've got nothing left to lose.' Poor cow."

The two officers stepped out of their car and joined Rachel and Michelle on their approach to the garage. Anderson emerged from the side gate carrying a spare tyre. As soon as he caught sight of them, he growled into the wind. Holding a bolt gun in his other hand, he strode over to the approaching police officers. "What the fuck is it now? I'm finishing after I've done this last job."

"Put that down, Mr. Anderson," Rachel commanded, pointing to the bolt gun. Anderson dropped the tyre and bolt gun with a scowl. She nodded to Matt, who took out his handcuffs. "Toby Anderson, I am arresting you on suspicion of attempting to pervert the course of justice. You do not have to say anything, but it may harm your defence if you do not mention, when questioned, something you later rely on in court. Anything you do say may be given as evidence. Do you understand?"

Anderson began to wriggle and pushed up against Matt, who gripped his wrist more firmly. Kev hooked his thick arms underneath Anderson's, pinning him up against the wall of the garage with a shudder.

"Stop it. Alright mate, I'll come quietly," Anderson yelled at Kev. Turning to Rachel, his red face glistening with sweat, he glared at her.

"Poppy, are you OK this afternoon? You don't quite seem yourself." Margaret clasped her wrinkly hands over her stomach as she approached the library's returns desk.

Snapping out of her daydream, Poppy half-smiled. "I'm just worried about Amanda. She didn't come home last night and she's not returning my calls. Her mother's alive and she's only got my voicemail to explain it to her. It must be hurting her so much to know her mother's out there but doesn't want to come home. She's all alone now." A look of determination and pride crossed Poppy's face as she turned to Margaret.

"But she's got me. All these years and I've not been much use to her. Now I can be. I can be a *proper* friend to her. I can be what she needs right now."

"Is that what *you* want, dear?" Margaret asked, her look quizzical. "I mean, I know you're staying a lot more at her house, to keep her company. I didn't mind so much at the start, when we thought something terrible had happened to Diana, you using the facilities here to spread the word. But now we know she's safe." She lay a hand on Poppy's arm. "I think it would be best for you to start concentrating more on work. I need your ideas to keep this place open. You just don't seem like my Poppy anymore." She looked Poppy up and down, noticing her tight jeans and designer long-sleeved t-shirt. "You're even wearing Amanda's clothes, aren't you?"

Pulling her arm away, Poppy scowled. "I'm just trying out a new style. What's the harm in that? She was only throwing these out anyway."

Margaret looked a little upset by Poppy's short tone. "Well, it's not really any of my business."

"Not really," Poppy murmured, then turned back to her book sorting.

RACHEL AND MICHELLE sat in the interview room opposite Anderson. The duty solicitor, dressed in a smart grey three piece suit, sat quietly next to him writing notes. Rachel had found that police interview rooms tended to be the same wherever you went in the country. Blandly painted walls, dirty carpets, solid tables that were bolted to the floor and chairs that were deliberately designed to be uncomfortable. Then there was the smell: cheesy feet mixed with ripe body odour.

"Let's get started, then," Rachel said, pressing the buttons on the tape recorder. "Detective Inspector Rachel Morrison and Police Constable Michelle Barlow in attendance with the suspect." Rachel paused. "Can you state your names for the tape, please?"

Anderson shuffled in his seat and folded his arms. "Toby Anderson," he mumbled.

"Philip Shaw," the duty solicitor stated, before returning to his note taking.

After stating the time, date, and location of the interview for the purpose of the tape, Rachel read, from the idiot card sellotaped to the scratched and dented desk in front of her, the other blurb about what would happen to the tapes and how he could get a copy of them should he be charged with an offence after the interview. After giving the caution and confirming with him that he understood it, she began with her first question.

"Mr. Anderson, can you tell us, please, why you lied about your whereabouts on the night Diana Walker was reported to have gone missing?" She clasped her hands together and rested them on the desk between them.

"No comment."

Michelle folded her arms. "We'll be here all night at this rate," she huffed under her breath.

Rachel continued unperturbed. "You said in your statement that on the night in question, you finished work at 6 p.m., like you do every evening, then went straight home to your fiancée. Are you still sticking with that?"

"No comment."

"See, your fiancée called us. Said you didn't come home until much later. Then you put your clothes in the washing machine before you'd even said 'hello'. Said it was very strange as you never wash your own clothes." Rachel made direct eye contact with the duty solicitor, who at that moment had looked up. "Your fiancée remembers it very clearly, as she didn't know you even knew *how* to switch on the washing machine."

"We have been granted authority under Section 18 of the

Police and Criminal Evidence Act 1984 to search your premises again, and the garage, Mr. Anderson, and I should warn you that officers are on their way there now to do exactly that," Michelle chipped in.

Anderson looked up. He swallowed hard and licked his dry lips.

"It's best for you if you tell us everything, Mr. Anderson," Rachel said.

With a huge exhale, Anderson slumped forward and buried his head in his hands. "OK. OK. I haven't been telling the truth."

Shaw clasped his elbow. "Toby, may I remind you of my earlier advice to make no comment at this stage." He turned to Rachel. "My client has…"

"It's OK. I want to tell them. I need to get it off my chest," Anderson said, removing his arm from his solicitor's clutches. "You want the truth? Here it is."

―――

AMANDA CLOSED the door to her room at the Anchor Pub and walked down the stairs. After handing in her room key to the bar, she took a deep breath and pulled up the zip to her coat. Walking along the same stretch of coastal path as she had done last night, she waited at the lighthouse door for the group to arrive. The Nurse was the first on the scene. Not wanting to seem too eager, Amanda waited for The Teacher to arrive, then finally The Gardener. He hadn't said much last night, so she was especially curious to hear his story. There was something she couldn't put her finger on about him, but all would be revealed tonight, she thought.

―――

RACHEL RETURNED to the police interview room with a fresh black coffee for Toby Anderson. He looked up and nodded his thanks before taking a thirsty sip. She inserted a brand new set of tapes into the machine and went through the introductions again, finishing with the caution.

"Mr. Anderson, if you'd like to continue your explanation as to why you lied about your whereabouts on the night of Diana Walker's disappearance," Michelle said.

Anderson licked his lips and cleared his throat. "The day when that woman, Diana Walker, came into the garage, I was having a really bad day. It was all kicking off, you know? Boss was giving me grief about being late again, my missus moaning about me not spending enough time with her. What am I supposed to do, eh? I'm late for work because she doesn't want to be alone, but I've gotta work to keep the roof over our heads and keep myself out of prison. It's a condition of my parole, you see? So I'm in a right foul mood, then she shows up in her fancy motor, flashing the cash and giving me attitude. I'm working on another job and she marches straight up to me and demands I take a look at her car. Said there'd been some damage done to it." Anderson wiped his face and cleared his throat again. "So, I take a look and sure enough there's a dirty great scratch all down one side. Like it's been keyed or something. I told her I hadn't done it, but she went on and on, saying she was gonna tell old Dixon. Get me sacked, like. I mean, how's that fair? I ain't done nothing. I'm not perfect, not at all, but I've been trying to keep my nose clean since coming out, trying not to fuck up, what with Becca, and the kiddie on the way, and here's this rich bitch trying to ruin everything for me."

"What happened next, Toby?" Rachel asked.

―――

"I'M GLAD YOU CAME BACK," The Nurse said as Amanda walked into the dark and dank basement of the lighthouse and into the same room they all sat in the previous night. The Teacher and Gardener followed closely behind.

"Yeah," Amanda replied.

The Nurse made everyone a mug of tea and ushered Amanda to a seat at the table. "Well, it's strange, us meeting up twice in two nights, but I think my husband bought my excuses. Teacher?"

The Teacher, more casually dressed this time in a dark blue hoodie and grey jeans, nodded. "Yeah. Said I was going the pub. Champions League's on, so I'm covered 'til at least 11 p.m. I'll Google the score later." He smiled and sipped his tea.

Amanda stared directly at The Gardener, who had remained quiet. "We didn't get time for you to tell me your story," she said.

"Or yours," he countered, not lowering his sharp brown eyes.

"You first. I'm nervous," Amanda shot back. She clasped her hands together underneath the table.

The Nurse let out a little laugh. "Come now, Daughter. Why don't you tell us a little bit about yourself first? How did you meet The Therapist?"

Amanda shot a glance at her. "I went to therapy because my mum thought I was going off the rails a bit after we moved here, and she said if I didn't go, she would stop my allowance. I hated it at first. Hated opening up to some stranger but I started to like it."

"I think we can all relate to that," The Teacher said.

"He's definitely made what we've done easier to live with. Even though what he's been through was worse." The Nurse reached over for the biscuits and began offering them out.

"That's one thing he never told me," Amanda said. "Why he was helping us all. Did he tell you?"

The Teacher nodded. "I asked him that. He said it was because he wanted 'justice for bad people'. His daughter, Sophie, was murdered a few years ago now. It was in all the papers at the time. She was only seventeen years old, for fuck's sake. Poor cow. She was set up by her friend, who was jealous Sophie was going out with her ex, and when this girl saw Sophie had tagged this place she was going one night on Instagram, she followed her there. Then at the end of the night, Sophie decided to walk home alone. Worst mistake she could have made. The girl followed her, then jumped her. Hit her over the head with a brick and dragged her into the bushes. She beat the shit out of poor Sophie."

"Shit," Amanda said.

"That's not the worst bit," The Teacher continued. "Before she left her there in those bushes, the bitch set Sophie on fire. The autopsy showed Sophie had ash in her lungs. She was still breathing while her fucking body was on fire. How fucked up is that? Anyway, because the killer was sixteen, shortly turning seventeen, her sentence was pathetic. Only five years in a pissing young offenders institute. Sophie was The Therapist's only child and he worshipped her. Imagine, your only kid being set on fire while they were alive."

The Nurse and The Gardener looked down at the table as The Teacher told the story, their eyes dim.

"So, The Therapist vowed that nobody else would ever go through that sense of injustice or pain ever again. Not if he could help it. He's made it his mission to eradicate scum from this town. And the country, even the world, if he could. He knows he can't do anything for his own daughter now, or get to her perpetrator. She was given a new identity, like they all are." He snorted in derision. "Even though he has money, and connections, he can't find Sophie's killer. Or who she is now. Maybe what he does for us all is his own healing process. Whatever the reason, he's taken care of my situation, and for that I'm loyal to the death to him."

"And me," The Nurse said, nodding.

"Me too," The Gardener piped up, breaking his silence. "I'm not proud of what I've done, but it needed doing. I couldn't stand back another day and watch what she was doing." He picked at the edge of the table until a large splinter of wood ripped off. At length he pulled it clear from the edge and fiddled with it. "She was no good. Always pushing people around 'cos she had a bit of money. I used to mow her lawn, you see? And prune the hedges, all that. But because she was rich she thought she could get away with hurting people. She had to go. Before she could do any more harm." He tried to lift his eyes to look at the others, but his shame stopped him.

"What was her name again?" The Nurse asked as she reached for a biscuit.

Taking a deep breath, Amanda leaned forward. "And where is she now?"

———

"I FUCKING hate myself for what I've done…" Anderson snivelled as he picked apart the polystyrene cup his coffee had come in over an hour ago. The duty solicitor looked on as Anderson lay his head down on the interview table and wrapped his arms around it.

Michelle shoved the box of tissues over to him. "Take your time."

Anderson lifted his head up and took a messy slurp from a beaker of water and wiped his nose on a tissue. "I left work at six, but Becca's right. I didn't go straight home."

"Where did you go, Toby?" Rachel asked.

"I don't deserve Becca after what I've done…she's gonna fucking leave me now."

"Toby?"

"I've been seeing somebody else. Of all people, I've been banging the boss's daughter." He looked up at Rachel and Michelle, then sideways at Shaw. "You can see now why I didn't wanna fucking advertise this. So after that woman, Diana, left, I was fuming. Becca has been having wild mood swings since she can't take her medication since being pregnant and, being honest, I couldn't deal with her. So that night,

I texted Stacey. We've been seeing each other for about six… seven weeks now. Known each other since I came out of prison, we have. She pops into the garage to see her dad now and then and, well, that's how we met. That night she asked me to come over after work, so I did. We shagged. A lot. It helped."

Rachel and Michelle looked sideways at each other.

Anderson continued. "Look, what do you want me to say, huh? I don't feel good about it. After I came home, I realised I stank of perfume and probably other stuff as you can imagine, so I put my clothes in the wash. I just said I'd got grease and shit on them. I think Becca is used to not asking me questions, not with my background. But the look on her face…that look on her fucking face…I've never felt guilt like it…and then she goes and sticks up for me with you lot. Believe it or not, I do have a conscience underneath."

Rachel's eyes narrowed. "So you're saying that you didn't go anywhere near Diana Walker or her property that night?"

"No. As God is my witness. Don't get me wrong, at the time I wanted to slap the woman silly, but after I got to Stacey's it was all forgotten about, trust me. I was more worried about hurting Becca and the boss not finding out. So, my head has been everywhere and the last thing I wanted was you guys sniffing around."

"We'll have to speak with Stacey, check your alibi," Michelle said. "What's her address?"

"I'm screwed, aren't I? I'll lose my job, my girl, and end up inside again." Anderson banged his head into his forearm on the desk.

"Better than being a murderer, though, isn't it?" Rachel said. "By the way, what brand of washing machine do you own, Toby?"

———

"I HAVE no idea where she is now. Why does that even matter?" The Gardener replied. He stood up and began pacing the stone floor of the lighthouse basement. "The Therapist took care of all of that. We didn't ask any more questions."

"But you must know?" Amanda pushed, her calm façade beginning to crack. The Nurse watched her, as did The Teacher.

"I think it's about time you told your story, Daughter," The Nurse said in an even tone. "You think we haven't worked out why you're here?"

Amanda's mouth went dry.

"We knew who you were as soon as you walked in. We saw you on the telly. The Teacher said, didn't he? We don't use names here. Usually. But there's something about you that seems a bit strange. You say you met The Therapist when you were going off the rails and your mother said she'd stop your allowance if you didn't go?"

"Yes," Amanda whispered.

"Is that why *you* wanted her to go missing?"

Amanda felt as if the air had been sucked completely out of the room. All eyes fixed on her. Before she could answer, a door in the corner of the room opened wide.

"What the *fuck* are you doing here, Amanda?" growled the tall, well-built figure standing in the doorway. He was wearing a dark hoodie and black combat pants. He looked to be in his mid-fifties, with thick black hair and a square jaw. His forehead was creased with deep lines as his face frowned at Amanda. The aura of a young frightened girl that had sat meekly at the table for the last two nights seemed to evaporate. Left behind was a cold stillness visible in the person everyone was now staring at, a sense of pure malevolence now pouring out of Amanda Walker.

"Nice to see you again," she purred. "I didn't realise you were the keyholder here. Nice cover."

"What's going on here?" The Gardener demanded.

The Therapist saw nobody else in the room other than Amanda. His stillness seemed incongruous to the rage and confusion displayed on his face.

"Daughter's one of our group, now," The Nurse said, looking at The Teacher and The Gardener. She frowned. "Isn't she?"

"No, she fucking isn't," The Therapist hissed.

Chapter 13

THREE HOURS after taking Anderson into the interview room, he was taken back before the custody sergeant to be released, pending further enquiries. Exhausted, Rachel headed back to her office, bumping into Superintendent Hargreaves on the way.

"Well? Did you speak to Little Miss Perfect?" Hargreaves asked.

"Poppy? No, not yet. We had a call from Becca Anderson on the way over there. We have to check out Toby Anderson's alibi, but I think we're barking up the wrong tree with that one. I doubt he'd admit to an affair, which could ruin him if it wasn't true." Rachel shook her head.

"You got anything else to go on?"

"No, just the washing machine noise on the train. But I'm going to speak to tech to see if there's any other explanation for that."

"So, Diana Walker *is* just wanting the world to leave her the fuck alone then?" Hargreaves said. "I want a confirmation from Amanda Walker that it *is* her mother's voice on that audio. Then I can get the press and that pain-in-the-arse MP to stop talking about this town as if it's the bloody Bermuda

Triangle. Has Diana Walker's payment to her brother gone out this month, by the way?"

Rachel shook her head and rubbed her tired eyes. "Not sure. I'll have to get my FI to check with the bank. That doesn't really prove anything, though; she does it by direct debit. Alive or dead, it'd still go out."

"True," Hargreaves conceded. "Right, well, tomorrow morning I want you to confirm with Amanda it's her mother's voice, then close this bloody case, Rachel."

"Ma'am."

———

UNDER THE DIM amber glow of the bulb in the lighthouse basement, The Therapist had been pacing the floor for a good few minutes before anyone could think of what to say.

"Look, is anyone going to tell us what the hell is going on?" The Gardener whined.

"Amanda is my client," The Therapist replied.

"We know that. But…" The Nurse said.

"She disclosed something to me in a session a while back." The Therapist screwed up his face and pinched the bridge of his nose. "Fuck. I've made a terrible error in judgement here."

"Shall I tell the story, doctor?" Amanda drawled, taking out her phone and pressing a couple of buttons. "You look a little…stressed."

The Therapist glared at her.

Amanda continued. "What he is trying to tell you all is, I once said in my therapy session that after a night of getting drunk and high on coke, I was driving back home through some country lanes at night. There was no lighting, and it was getting dark. All of a sudden, *smack*. I saw something fly through the air and into the bushes. I thought I'd hit an animal. I stopped the car and staggered out. I was so annoyed when I saw the damage to my car and thought, fucking hell, I've killed a deer or something. So, I looked through the bushes. Got scratched up, I can tell you. And then I saw what I'd hit." Amanda paused for effect. "A bloke. He was about twenty-three…twenty-four maybe? He was barely alive, but he looked right at me. He couldn't move, his back must have been broken or something, and he was bleeding from his nose, ears and mouth. So I knew it wasn't good." Pausing again, Amanda took a huge slurp of her tepid tea.

"My God. What happened to him?" The Nurse gasped.

Amanda looked her straight in the eye. "I watched him die. And I loved every. Single. Second of it."

There were gasps around the table, followed by a stunned silence. The Therapist looked down at his heavy black boots and squinted his eyes shut.

"You left him to die? How could you?" The Nurse said, tears now clogging up her eyes.

"Morbid curiosity, I guess," Amanda replied. She picked a biscuit crumb out of a back tooth. "It was fascinating to watch him take his last breath, me being the last thing he saw. I thought of what he must have been like when he was six, ten, eighteen years old. His friends who were missing him, and me knowing exactly where he was and knowing I could end it or prolong it. It was almost spiritual. Like I was God or something? Not that I believe in that shit, but it was…almost over *too* quick. I wanted to replay it. I wished I could have woken him up, let him run, then knocked him over again. My mind went all over the place with the possibilities."

"That's sick. What the fuck?" The Gardener said, looking at The Therapist, who had nothing but regret etched all over his face.

"Yep," Amanda continued. "I stayed with him for a bit after that. Watched the colour change in his face. Wasn't long before he became cold and I thought, I wonder who might be missing him tonight? A girlfriend, his mum…what would they give to switch places with me right now to hear his last breath. I felt fucking amazing. It was more of a high than the coke."

The Nurse put her hand to her mouth and began weeping. "That poor man."

The Gardener banged his fists into the desk and stood up. "You're not *anything* like us, you fucking twisted bitch," he yelled, stabbing a finger at Amanda, who smirked. "Who the fuck are you? Really?"

"It gets better…" Amanda replied, grinning. "You think *that's* twisted? You wait until you hear what I did next." She reached over for another biscuit and munched down on it.

"You're fucked up, you are!" The Gardener exclaimed.

"What do you mean, 'it gets better'? Who are you?" The Teacher stood up and walked over to Amanda's side of the table. She barely flinched.

"You're a monster. How could you do such a cruel thing?" The Nurse wiped her eyes with a balled up tissue from her sleeve.

"Cruel?" She tilted her head from side to side, weighing up the accuracy of that estimation. "Maybe? But I didn't know him, so who knows, he could have deserved it. Been a horrible boss, or a kiddie fiddler or something? But is that important? Are you saying that what you did was any better just because you decided that they deserved to die? We are all the same." There was a pause. "Perhaps not the same. There was one difference." She waited. The atmosphere was thick. "I didn't half enjoy it." Amanda let out a bark of laughter that made The Nurse jump.

"This isn't funny."

"What? I'm just being honest." Amanda looked at The Therapist. "It aroused *such* a curiosity in me to do it again." She then turned her head and flashed the others a look of pure evil. "And that's where you all came in. Because of our mutual friend over there," she said, cocking her head at The Therapist.

All three looked at The Therapist. To their surprise, he had tears in his steel grey eyes.

"What is it you want, Amanda?" The Therapist asked in a measured voice.

"To know where the burying place is. Where do you get rid of the bodies?" There was barely a tone in Amanda's ice cold question.

"Amanda, they don't know. Neither do I. I had someone take care of that part. It protects everyone. You should go. You're wasting your time here."

"Why on earth would you want to know where the bodies are *buried*? I'm so confused. Are you a journalist or something?" She looked around. "Are you the police? Is this a… a…bust?"

"Why do I want to know?" Amanda laughed. "Fascination, yeah, is a big factor. But mostly, because I need to know where I'm going to bury my mother. Eventually."

The mug The Nurse was holding dropped to the concrete floor, shattering into pieces.

"I don't want to get caught now, do I? I've done so well so far," Amanda added with a sly smile.

"You need to start talking. Now," The Teacher commanded, his face pale as he glared at The Therapist.

"Your mother's been missing for nearly two weeks now?" The Nurse asked, looking confused as she tried to piece together the fragments of Amanda's tale. "There's been no sightings of her, so I hear from the news." She stopped and looked at The Therapist. "Why don't you know anything about her mother's disappearance?"

Before he could answer, Amanda let out a chilling laugh.

"Clearly, you all haven't been paying attention. Haven't you worked it out yet? *I've* had my mother locked up for the last two weeks, while I've been trying to find you lot."

Stunned silence filled the room. Amanda continued.

"I went to the pub you all meet in. All I had to do to find you was Google 'pubs with dodgy reputations in the area.'

The Anchor has a reputation of being a haven of wrong'uns. While I was there, a news bulletin came on, about all the people that have gone missing, and when I asked the barman about your cosy, and very odd-looking, little group meeting going on in the corner, he sang like a canary. And you know what? He was right. A geeky-looking teacher, a middle-aged nurse and a, may I say, very fit looking gardener, all meet up in a pub. It's like the start of a bad joke. I mean, in what world would you bunch of misfits all be friends? So, I followed you all here and tricked you into blabbing. How you haven't been arrested and locked away is beyond me. You're all so fucking bad at this game. And unless you really *do* need me to spell it out for you, *I'm* the one who killed the three bastards you wanted rid of. Me. We all got what we wanted. I wanted the buzz of killing again, and you wanted those scumbags dead. And The Therapist could make it happen. So, really you should be thanking me. And it was so well run. Whoever does the clean-up, fair play to him. I shit myself after I did in the first one, that doctor. I thought I'd get a knock on the door five minutes later, but nothing. All I want in return is to know where to bury my mother, so I'm as free as a bird afterwards, like you all are. I'm only asking for one fucking thing from you." She scowled at The Therapist. "Now, Richard. It's very simple. I need to know who you hired to clear up the scene after I had killed them and where those bodies are buried. You know, Richard. So don't you be fucking telling me you don't. I'm on a time limit here, and I'm not doing all that shit for you lot and none of you wanna do fuck all for me."

The Nurse looked shell-shocked. "But your mother, Amanda? She doesn't sound like a monster. This is *completely* different to our cases." She took a seat next to Amanda and softened her voice. "It's not what we are about or why this group was created. We're traumatised every day for playing a part in ending a person's life. But that person was terrorising people. Your mother, what did she do to deserve this happening to her?"

Amanda's eyes darkened as she stared back at The Nurse. "So what you are saying is that if *you* decide someone deserves to die it's OK, but if I decide then it's murder? Who made you judge and jury? Anyway, my mother *does* deserve all that's coming to her. She's the one responsible for my dad's death."

"What? How?"

"He killed himself. She drove him to do it. She drove him to drink and that's when he did it. He was drunk that night…"

The Nurse shook her head. "This sounds like grief talking. You're angry. I get that, but you can't take your mother's life because of it. You'd be an orphan. Is that what you want?"

"You're fucking right I'm angry." Amanda stood up and paced the floor. "And how does my mum help me through my feelings? The night I run over the guy, I come back home and as soon as she sees me, my mum threatens to turn me over to the police right there and then for being drunk and high on coke. What kind of mother does that? Can you imagine what would happen if the police looked into my whereabouts that night? I'd get done for drunk driving and taking drugs, kicked out the house and also arrested for the *small matter* of killing some guy on the way home."

"Look, I'm sure your mother cares about you. She was probably frightened of losing you to the drink and drugs and wanted to teach you a lesson. My God, Amanda. What have you done?" The Therapist said.

Amanda remained unmoved. She walked up to The Therapist. "Richard, that's enough of this bullshit now. Where are those other three people buried?"

The Therapist raised his hands in surrender. "I don't know. I really don't know, Amanda."

"Then who does? I want a name."

"You know I can't tell you. I *won't* tell you."

Amanda clenched her jaw tight. "OK, have it your way. But I guess I'll have to sort it, with or without your help."

"What do you mean?" Richard asked, concerned.

Amanda laughed. "Well, I'll bury her in the best place I

can find and *hope* she's never found. But if I get taken down, you lot are *all* fucking coming with me, don't worry about that. Or, you tell me who gets rid of the bodies, we get them to do one last job for us *all*, as a returning favour to me for everything I've done for you snivelling fucktards, and we *all* stay out of the shit?" Amanda gave The Therapist one last long look. "Now, tell me where the burying place is."

No one moved, blinked or even breathed for what felt like an unnatural amount of time. The ceiling light swayed as a gust of wind swept up around the lighthouse. The window shutters a few floors above them clattered together with a hollow thud.

"So, you're blackmailing us? Is that why you're here?" The Gardener forced the words through his tight lips.

Amanda leaned back in her chair. "If you want to put it like that, then yes. I guess I am. But what the fuck do you care? Who the fuck are you to be all moral now?" The grin on Amanda's face was chilling.

"This isn't normal," The Nurse spluttered. "We are tormented every single day. We don't enjoy this. This isn't a high for us. We are looking over our shoulder to see if, for whatever reason, today is the day we get found out and not only is our life wrecked but so are our families. That constant worry is paralysing. Our reasons were genuine. Our people were bad people. Your mother is completely innocent. What you've done is barbaric." She got up from her chair and pointed at Amanda. "You're not right in the head."

Amanda looked down the barrel of The Nurse's outstretched finger. "You were happy for me to kill the kiddie fiddler though, weren't you? I looked him up before I did it. Richard gave me some basic details. I was curious. He looked like he had a *perfect* little life on Facebook. All for show, of course. So, I took care of it for you. But *now* you have a problem with morals?"

"It's not the same. Your mother is *not* the same. You can't go around playing God," The Nurse shrieked back.

"To you, maybe not. But in my eyes she's worse than all of your victims put together."

The Therapist sat down opposite Amanda and looked into her eyes. "How long has your mother been locked up, Amanda? Is she hurt?"

"Not as hurt as I want her to be." Amanda leaned forward and met his gaze across the table. "Who are the guys I need to speak to? I want her gone. Believe me, it's in all of your interests for me to get rid of her properly."

"What if we don't comply, Amanda? What if we deny everything?" The Nurse asked, her voice trembling.

"When the police question me I'll play them this audio." She held up her phone and flashed a smile of accomplishment. "I've been recording you lot spilling your little secrets. Including how you gave the go-ahead to get somebody murdered. This here is cast iron evidence you've known all this time they were not *missing*, they are rotting somewhere."

There was a sudden rush of hands scrabbling across the table trying to snatch the phone off Amanda, who drew her hand away to safety, tucking it underneath her now folded arms.

"You nasty little bitch!" The Nurse exclaimed.

"For fuck's sake, Amanda!" The Therapist yelled.

Amanda looked down at the phone and pressed a few buttons. Looking up, she smirked. "And yes, I did just email it to myself, so if anything happens to me, it will be found anyway once the police start investigating my disappearance. You're all fucked."

The Teacher looked at The Therapist. "For fuck's sake, Richard, what do we do now?"

The Therapist looked at Amanda, who seemed to have zoned out momentarily. "Amanda? Amanda." She looked back at him. "I'm going to need some time. To contact these people. Can you give me at least that? One of them is out of town until the weekend."

"You have three days. I'll come back here then. And you

all need to be here too." She pointed around the room. "Richard, you will have names for me. Or *I* will do it myself, then have names of my own for the police, you understand?" She got up from her chair. "I'll see myself out."

———

IT WAS a good minute or so before anyone could speak after Amanda had left the lighthouse.

"I think I'm going to be sick," The Nurse said, her face pale.

"Richard, what the fuck…you got *her* to do it of all fucking people?" The Teacher glared in disbelief at The Therapist.

"Well, there's not exactly a directory of assassins on Google. It had all gone to plan. We *had* actually all got away with it, remember. Then it went quiet and the police left it alone. Then, fuck me, Amanda snaps."

"Well, did you expect her to be a well-adjusted young lady?" The Nurse exclaimed. "After recruiting her from a therapy session, in which she disclosed the fact that she enjoyed killing somebody, to murder people for us? She's a bloody psycho. You are responsible for this…you. What a fuck-up. My husband… Oh God, the stress of this will kill him." She ran her hands through her short hair and wiped her eyes.

"You need to get in touch with these people, Richard. You need to do what she says, or we're all sunk," The Teacher whined.

"Are you serious?" The Gardener said. "There's an innocent woman locked up somewhere, someone who's done nothing wrong, and we're actively going to help this psychopath Amanda dispose of her body after she murders her? And we're OK with this?"

"Of course not. But what options do we have?" The Teacher replied, throwing his head into his hands. "I can't go down. I've got a wife too. If she ever finds out what I've done, what I have to live with every single day…"

The Gardener slammed his fist down on the table, making the cups rattle. "What we did, we did for the greater good. To save lives and pain in the long run. That girl is a monster. Killing for kicks. If we do this, if we help her, we become exactly the same as her."

Chapter 14

"Morning, boss. Breakfast?" Michelle said, handing Rachel a coffee and brown bag. "Having a tidy up?"

Rachel put down the pile of folders she'd packed up from her desk and sighed. "Yeah. I just... Don't you think it seems like a strange case? I mean, Hargreaves wanted us to take the lead rather than the Misper Unit, but now we're finally starting to get somewhere she wants us to give it back to them and move onto something else. I think I want to speak to Amanda. See how she is. It should really come from me that we're not looking into her mother's case anymore and that someone else will be taking over. She'll be fuming."

"Maybe. But if her mother wants to get away and spend some time dealing with her shit, then maybe it's just as well that Amanda learns to deal with it. Get on with her own life. It's not like she's poor, is it?"

"True. I'll eat this, then go over there." Rachel pulled her croissant out of the bag and took a bite. Her desk phone rang just as she was swallowing. "Morrison."

"It's Andy, down at AV. We've had a hit on the people who bought the same make and model of washing machine we heard on the tape."

Rachel covered the mouthpiece. "Shit. I forgot to tell the

AV guys we were passing the baton to Missing Persons," she whispered to Michelle. "Go on, Andy, tell me what you found."

"Well, after we confirmed that Anderson's washing machine made a different tune, we took a look at who else in the local area bought the same make and model of machine we were looking for. We got a hit. Very local. Very familiar name. You're not gonna believe who has one like this."

"Andy, spit it out. I'm not getting any younger," Rachel said, chewing on the last of her croissant.

"A machine of the same make and model as the one heard on the AV of Diana Walker saying to leave her alone…was sold to Diana Walker."

Rachel nearly choked on a crumb of pastry. "Are you certain?"

"100%."

"Shit. Thanks, Andy." Rachel looked over at Michelle, both eyebrows raised. "The plot thickens."

"OK. What does that mean?" Michelle asked as Rachel pulled out of the police car park. They had just received the update on the cell site they had requested and it showed Diana's call had been made from within the radius of the cell covering the home address. That, coupled with the audio of the dishwasher playing in the background, made it seem fairly conclusive to Rachel that Diana had made the call from within her own house.

"Well, there are two things that strike me as odd," Rachel said, trying to marshal her thoughts. "Firstly, she's been missing for two whole weeks and in that time no one has seen hide nor hair of her, so why did she suddenly decide to return home? Secondly, why would she ring us from her house and then claim to be on a train when she clearly wasn't?"

"She could just have been waiting for an opportunity to

come back when she knew Amanda was definitely going to be out in order to collect some personal things," Michelle pointed out. "And maybe she didn't say she was at home because she knew we would rush straight around and she didn't want to see us."

The suggestions were perfectly reasonable and made a great deal of sense, Rachel accepted, but she had long ago learned to trust her instinct, and right now it was telling her that something was not right.

"We need to talk to Amanda, try and find out what her mother's state of mind was the last time she saw her," she said. "I'm worried that Diana is planning to do something silly."

―――

As THEY ARRIVED at the Walker property and pulled into the driveway, Rachel noticed that Amanda's car was parked in its usual space.

"She's back then. That's a relief," Michelle said.

They walked up to the front door and rang the bell. Amanda appeared. She wore a baggy jumper and jogging bottoms. Her eyes had large dark circles underneath them, her hair lacking its usual lustre.

"Hi, Amanda. Can we come in?" Rachel asked.

"Sure. But I'll be honest, I'm not feeling so good. I'm not really sleeping and I have this headache…"

"It won't take a minute. Can we come in?"

Amanda shrugged and pushed the door wide enough for Rachel and Michelle to squeeze past. In the kitchen, Poppy was making two cups of coffee.

"Oh…hello officers. Would you like a coffee?" Poppy smiled as she popped a pod into the coffee machine.

"No thank you, Poppy. We just came to play Amanda the audio we have." Rachel fished her phone out of her jacket pocket.

"Poppy told me about it," Amanda said. "Sorry I wasn't

available to confirm for you. I've been feeling very down lately and I just needed some space. I'm sure Poppy's right. It probably is my mother on that tape. I'm just really upset that she has left me on my own. Who would do that to their own daughter? It's a lot to take in and I'm trying my best to."

"All the same, I'd like to play it to you. If that would be OK? It won't upset you too much, will it?" Rachel asked, unmoved by Amanda's emotional state.

"Upset me? Why? Because it proves my mother isn't dead. She's just left me alone, like my father did. I just have to deal with it." The sarcasm dripped from Amanda, so much so that it startled Rachel. Throughout the playback of the audio, Amanda's face remained completely impassive. "That's her," she confirmed.

"Don't you think there's just something a little different about her voice, Mand?" Poppy piped up.

"It's her. And no. I don't." Amanda shot a hard look at Poppy, who flinched.

"Can I ask where your washing machine is, please?" Rachel asked.

Both Poppy and Amanda stared at Rachel, bewildered by her completely random question.

"Why?" Amanda replied. Rachel raised an eyebrow at the lack of a simple yes.

"Just something I need to check," Rachel replied.

Amanda led Rachel and Michelle over to the utility room. As they approached the washing machine, Michelle noted down the make and model.

"It's the right one, boss," Michelle said, nodding. She took out her phone and snapped a picture of it.

"I don't understand." Amanda said, folding her arms.

"Well, you see, when your mother made that call, there was the very distinctive tune of a washing machine coming to the end of its cycle. We checked it out with our tech guys and, as it turns out, this one you have here is exactly the same make and model as the one on the tape. Your mum made that call to us with the washing machine in the background. It was only faint. But as you heard her say on the tape, she was on a train. Can you think of why she would say she was somewhere different than where she actually was?"

Amanda shook her head and led them back into the kitchen, absent-mindedly picking things up and putting them down again. "Maybe her head wasn't right and she meant she was *about* to board a train?"

"Hmm…maybe," Rachel nodded. "But we checked all the CCTV. There was no sign of your mother in any stations boarding any trains. It's almost as if she was in this house one minute, then after that she's not seen again. It's a complete mystery."

Amanda held Rachel's inquisitive stare for a moment, then looked away and shrugged again. "I bet they've sold loads of that make of washing machine. It's probably coincidence. Anyway, you're the detective. You work it out."

Both Michelle and Rachel noticed a change in Amanda's body language.

"Amanda, I need you to check the house and see if any of your mother's belongings are missing: stuff that was here when you reported her missing a couple of weeks ago but has vanished since your mother called to us."

Amanda bristled, but didn't say anything. With a huff, she went off to check, returning a few minutes later. "Not that I can tell, but I can't say for sure."

"How are you coping, Amanda?" Rachel asked.

"OK, I guess. Considering I now know my own mother doesn't want to be here with me anymore. Charming, that." Amanda took a long drink from her coffee. "Would be just typical if she *did* turn up dead now, after all my efforts to try and find her. But thank you, detective inspector, and you, PC Barlow, for all you've done to help. And I just want you to know that I won't blame you, or your department, if my mother *is* found one day at the bottom of a cliff. Maybe that's what she wanted after all. I have to accept that."

Poppy put her arm around Amanda's shoulders, but Amanda's changed demeanour pricked at Rachel.

―――

"You OK?" Michelle asked after noticing Rachel hadn't said a word since they left the Walker residence.

"Don't you think it was weird? I mean, how would you be if your mum said she wanted to be away from everybody, including you?"

Michelle frowned. "Devastated. Angry. Why?"

"There wasn't even a flicker of anger from Amanda. Just a coldness. It's like she wasn't surprised. I mean, her mother had just upped and left, without even a 'see ya later'? Now, I don't know about you, but if my mum had done that I'd be *livid*. At one point Amanda must have thought she was dead. Then when we get proof she's alive, Amanda's not even the slightest bit angry she'd been led to believe the worst? And don't forget, her mum decides to ring the local police, not her. That must hurt. She sounded more pissed off with her, to be honest."

"People deal with trauma in different ways. What are you thinking?" Michelle replied.

"I don't know. Just seems a bit odd. Remember what she was like at the press conference? All tears when she thought her mum was missing. Now, not even a flicker."

"Reckon she knows more about this than she's letting on?"

"I'm starting to think so, yeah," Rachel said, shaking her head.

"Great. Hargreaves is gonna love us even more now," Michelle replied.

―――

Amanda drummed her fingers on the white marble kitchen counter as Poppy busied herself at the sink. It had been ten minutes since Rachel and Michelle had left the house.

"I'm not meaning to sound funny, Pops, but how long were you thinking of staying?"

Poppy turned round, looking slightly hurt. "Oh, but I thought I could make us some dinner after I've washed up these cups."

"I've texted Max, asked him to stay the night. I mean, we have found out that my mum is OK. She just doesn't want to be with me, but it's fine. I'll cope somehow," Amanda replied.

"I see. Sorry, I just assumed, with the news about your mum and everything, that you'd want some company."

"I do. Max." Amanda's tone hardened, as did her stare.

"Right. You've hardly spoken about Max or seen him, so I didn't know if that was all going OK. Well, I'll leave you to it then." Poppy folded the tea towel neatly and laid it on the counter. "But call me if you need anything. Promise?"

"Promise," Amanda replied, looking down at her phone as Poppy left.

As soon as Amanda heard the front door close, she rose and walked over to it. She deadlocked it and threaded the chain across. Walking back into the kitchen, she locked the back door and pulled the blind down. After filling a plastic beaker with water, she took a pre-packaged sandwich out of the fridge and headed towards the utility room. Placing the beaker and sandwich on the counter, she lifted the rug below her, revealing a cellar hatch, around three feet square. Pulling at the silver ring, the hatch rose. Inside was a set of wooden steps. Amanda picked up the beaker and sandwich and descended the steps.

"No point making any noise. It's just you and me here now. I finally got rid of Poppy."

She reached the bottom and stood staring at the pathetic sight of her mother bound to a rickety wooden chair and gagged, her head lolled to the side. Her usually pristine makeup was now smeared all over her face and had mixed with her terrified tears. Her once perfectly curled shoulder length brown hair was now flat and dull, and matted around her temples from sweat. She was still very drowsy from the latest dose of drugs that she had been forced to take. Amanda had soundproofed the room as best she could, but it wasn't perfect. Drugging her mother when she went out or she was expecting anyone to come around to the house was her only option. Diana Walker mumbled her reply and opened her eyes, red from the dust and the grime from the musty wine cellar air, but with remnants of fight still in them.

"What's that, Mother dearest? Can't quite make out what you said there?" Amanda mocked. "That was a close one, phew. Had the coppers walking just above your head just then. Good thing they never stood on the rug, otherwise they'd have felt the hatch. But, they're closing the missing person case on you now. Now that you've called in to say you're safe and well. They did say you didn't sound yourself though, but I'm not sure how *they* would sound having a five-inch knife against their throat as they were speaking, but still…"

Amanda smirked and stepped closer to her mother. She removed the gag and fed her the sandwich. Diana took a hungry bite, almost choking with the dryness of her throat. Seeing this, Amanda gave her a sip of the water.

"So, tell me, how does it feel to know that there isn't a soul now looking for you? How does it feel to be left completely alone? Not very nice, is it?"

"Amanda, please. Just let me go. I won't say anything. I'll pretend I just went away for a while. Please. You don't have to do this." Diana Walker's voice was thin, desperate. Fresh tears began to trace themselves down the streaks already there on her sweaty face.

"Don't worry. You won't be down here for much longer." Amanda smiled as a look of relief drifted over her mother's face, knowing she was about to shatter it. "Once I find out where to dump your body, you'll be out of here."

Amanda replaced the gag, stifling her mother's anguished cry, then ascended the steps without another word. She closed the hatch, plunging Diana once again into darkness.

Chapter 15

"How do you think she'll take it?" Michelle asked, as they walked over to Hargreaves' office from their desks. It was just after 6 p.m. and everyone else had already gone home.

"Soon find out," Rachel replied, knocking.

"Come in," came the usual harsh bark from inside.

Rachel pushed the door open and saw Hargreaves sitting at her desk. "Ma'am. I know I'm supposed to be closing the Diana Walker case…"

Hargreaves let out a long exhale. "I thought I made myself perfectly clear on that one."

"Yes. You did. But there's just something niggling me still."

Hargreaves took off her glasses and fixed Rachel with a weary, but sharp, stare. "For fuck's sake, Rachel, I need you on other cases. Let this one go. It's sorted."

"Call it copper's instinct, but I just need another day or so. I'd like to have a look at the CCTV from the immediate surrounding area of the Walker house."

"I thought we'd reviewed all that?" Hargreaves replied.

"The footage of the train stations, Anderson's garage and the roads in between." Rachel paused and looked back at Michelle who took out her notepad. "But we didn't look at the security camera right above Diana's front door. Or the one fixed above the side gate."

Hargreaves sat forward in her chair. "I wasn't aware there *was* a camera on the property."

"Neither was I. It's only small and Amanda didn't mention it. I noticed it just now when we left the Walker premises. It's only tiny, the one above the gate. And the one on her door is one of those new doorbell cameras. The ones that tell you the postman's been."

"What are you thinking, Rachel?" Hargreaves asked, her hard stare softening into an inquisitive look.

"I want to know when, and more importantly *if*, Diana Walker actually walked out of that house prior to her daughter reporting her missing."

Hargreaves thought it over for a second. "What? You think she's under the patio or something? Whatever's going on here, I need answers because I want this bloody case wrapped up sharpish." Hargreaves sighed. "OK, I get that you have a gut feeling about this case, but I can't keep throwing resources at something that might not even be a crime. I'll give you a couple more days and then that's it. If there's a crime going on, solve it; if not, hand it over to the Misper Unit. I mean it, Rachel."

Rachel smiled. "Yes, ma'am."

"Now both of you, go home and get some rest. If I know that look on your face, DI Morrison, this case is *far* from over."

Back at their desks, Michelle grabbed her police jacket and logged off her computer. "You coming out for a drink with us all tonight? You missed the last one, remember?"

Rachel shook her head. "No, not tonight. Adam's bringing home a curry, so..."

"Oooh, very nice," Michelle said, winking. "Have a good night. See you tomorrow."

"Night, Michelle."

Once she'd gone, Rachel fished out her phone and called Adam's number. Sighing, she waited for the beep. "Hi… It's me," she began. "Look…I just wanted you to know, I know what I did. And I'm sorry. I totally understand now when you said I was getting too involved in cases. I guess I just can't help myself. It takes its toll on those around me, and I get that now. I'm different now. Since losing our baby I…" Rachel paused, wiping her eyes with her palm. "I know I hurt you, and I know what happened was all my fault. The stuff I did. I'm so sorry. Please, just call me back, Adam. We can work this all out, but we need to talk. I miss you."

Rachel pressed the end call button. Before she put the phone back in her jacket, a message from her mum popped up. Before she'd even thought about it, she'd texted back, declining her mother's invite for dinner.

―――

"Max, hi," Amanda said after opening her front door to him. She smiled as he stood on the grey stone doorstep, the yellowy porch light bouncing off his chiselled cheekbones.

"I came straight over. I'm so glad you texted. Mum's got the dog tonight, so I can stay as long as you want me to. I've missed you. You haven't been returning my calls recently, so I was beginning to think…" Max swept his dark hair out of his chocolate brown eyes and blushed. "Anyway. Here." He thrust a huge bunch of flowers towards Amanda, who took them reluctantly. "You look amazing, by the way," Max gushed, looking her up and down, her tight red dress mesmerising him.

"You didn't have to go to such an effort, Max," she replied, looking down at the flowers with disdain. Max, completely oblivious to Amanda's reaction, smiled and smoothed down his freshly pressed purple shirt. "Come in then."

Max shimmied past Amanda and walked into the kitchen.

"Drink?" Amanda asked, dumping the flowers on the counter.

"Erm…well, I brought this." Max showed her a bottle of screw-top Chardonnay.

Amanda wrinkled her nose.

"But, well, maybe you've got something better down in the cellar. I'll go check, shall I? You always say you hate going down there. Don't worry, I'll get the spiders." Max stepped towards the wine cellar hatch, but Amanda grabbed his arm.

"No. It'll be fine. I'll put it in the fridge to cool." She pulled him away from the hatch area by wrapping her arms around him. "Besides, I don't need alcohol to warm me up tonight. I'm not wearing any knickers." She grabbed his free hand and slid it up her dress, biting her lip as he gasped.

"OK then," Max said. "But I really don't mind if you'd rather just chill together tonight? We could get a pizza in, have that crap wine?" He smiled again at his own joke, but Amanda's face sank into a sultry stare. She took the wine bottle from him and placed it on the counter.

"No way. I've got plans for you tonight."

Half-dragging Max upstairs, tearing at his shirt, she kissed him and ran her hands through his thick dark hair. Reaching the bedroom, they flopped onto Amanda's huge bed.

"I've really missed you," Max whispered as he stroked Amanda's cheek. "I would have been here. I called, but you never picked up."

"You're here now." Amanda smiled and kissed him. Then a darkness seemed to cross her eyes. She rolled over him and pinned his arms above his head. "And I intend to make it up to you." She sank her face into his neck, her slow tender kisses turning hotter after each one. Kisses turned to nibbles, then into bites.

"Ouch," Max said, wincing. "That one hurt a bit. Go slow, will you. We've got all night."

"No," Amanda replied. "I'm hungry for you." With pure lust in her eyes, she lowered her hands and began unbuckling his jeans. Yanking them down, she then hooked her fingers under his Calvin Kleins and peeled them away from his trembling hips. "I know you've wanted me to do this for a while now, so…" She lowered her face onto him, taking him inside her mouth.

Max gasped. "Oh my God, Amanda." He clasped his hands around her head. "I don't think it's gonna be long…" His voice tailed off as he laid his head back.

As he edged closer to his climax, Amanda stopped. She lifted her head up and wiped her mouth. "Not yet, you don't." She reached over and opened the top drawer of her bedside table, taking out a pair of silver handcuffs. She grabbed Max's wrists and secured them to the wooden slats of her headboard.

"Amanda, we've never done this before," Max panted. "You seem…*different*."

Amanda put her lips to his ear. "Well, you get to fuck two different Amandas tonight then, don't you, you lucky boy." She took out a silk scarf from underneath the pillow and wrapped it around his head, tying it in a tight bow. "It's about time we spiced things up. And I'm feeling horny tonight." She raked her fingernails down his bare chest, leaving long red trails. "Imagine how tragic it would be, dying without ever having the wildest night of your life?"

"Amanda, you're scaring me a little bit." Max's voice quivered as he wriggled, completely prone with his hands cuffed above his head and Amanda pinning his legs down as she straddled him.

Max heard the unmistakable sound of a match being struck. The next thing he felt was a searing pain as heavy blobs of liquid dropped onto his bare chest. Drip after drip after drip. Through the tiny gap by his nose, Max saw Amanda holding a lit candle.

"The pain only lasts a second," she purred. "Then you feel euphoric. Like you can take anything that touches you."

"Amanda, stop. I'm not enjoying this."

Amanda ignored him and pressed her palm into his wax-covered chest. "Stop being a pussy, Max. It's just a little fun. Get a grip and live a little, will ya?"

"It's not fun. It hurts. Can you let me go now?"

"I'm having fun."

Amanda sank lower and took him inside her mouth again, sending him into a writhing mix of pleasure and pain as she pinched at his balls with her nails. Again, moments later, she stopped.

"Fuck's sake, Amanda," he groaned.

"Oh, I've only just begun with you."

Seconds later, Max let out an ear piercing scream.

"Thank God we live in a detached house," Amanda said.

"Take this off me now!" Max screamed breathlessly, wriggling his head to try and remove the blindfold. "I wanna know what you just did that hurt so much."

With one hand, Amanda took off his blindfold and saw tears in his beautiful brown eyes. These eyes widened in horror when they saw the ten-inch carving knife Amanda was holding.

"Jesus Christ!" Max cried. He looked down at his chest, where now there were thin streaks of blood running in between the now-dry blobs of candle wax. It was a mess, but Amanda laughed.

"Sex games. It's just me branding you. Nothing life threatening. Yet," she added.

"Amanda… This ain't right. This is fucked up. I never had you down for doing this shit."

"Well, maybe I can change that for you," Amanda said. Hitching her dress up, she positioned herself just right, then sank down on him, moaning as he entered her. "How about now?"

Max groaned also and bucked his hips, but again she pinned him back down. "Amanda, no."

Max closed his eyes and grimaced, the feeling of what Amanda was doing almost unbearable mixed with the blistering pain from his chest. Feeling her rise and fall on top of him, over and over again, made every second harder to bear, until Amanda began to pant, now riding him hard. Finally, she cried out, her own climax reached. Max looked up in her direction as she pulled his exhausted manhood out of herself.

A long ten seconds later, she pressed her palms down on the wounded parts of his chest and kissed him hard. "Now you can come," she whispered into his open mouth. When he didn't out of terror, Amanda used her hand to help move things along. Moments later it was all over.

"I need to get a shower now," Amanda said, looking down at her wet thigh. She unclipped his handcuffs and threw them back on the bedside table. "You can let yourself out, can't you?"

"Wait, what?" Max stuttered. He shook his head in confusion.

"You tell your mates about that and you'll be a fucking hero." Amanda walked towards the ensuite. She turned to look back at him. "Look, let me get a wet cloth and I'll clean up your chest. It's not as bad as it looks."

"Don't fucking bother. Fucking hell, look at the state of me," Max replied. He reached down to the side of the bed for his clothes and dressed as quickly as he'd been stripped.

"Suit yourself," Amanda said, leaving him to finish tying his shoelaces as she closed the bathroom door behind her.

Chapter 16

Rachel gripped the steering wheel and wrenched it to the left, swerving the car across the road to a halt, narrowly missing the Fiesta that had suddenly cut across her path.

"Fuck's sake!" she exclaimed. "I should bloody book you for that."

The other driver waved furiously back. As she was about to get out of her car to give him an earbashing, Rachel looked up through her windscreen and saw the no entry sign bearing down on her. Realising her mistake, she nodded her apology and backed up.

"Get a grip, Morrison," she chastised herself as she rubbed her eyes to wake herself up fully.

Making it to the station without any more incidents, she bumped into Michelle who was carrying her usual coffee order.

"I got you a double shot," Michelle said, smiling. "You're gonna need it when you find out how much CCTV footage we've gotta wade through."

"I just want the footage from the doorbell camera, and the one on the fence if possible?" Rachel replied, taking her coffee and swigging it.

"I know, but have to get permission from Amanda for that, and also the neighbour next door whose fence she shares. There's a public security camera on the lamp post near the Walker's property. I thought if we got that it might save us another visit to Amanda. I'm pretty sure she's sick of us by now. It can't be easy for her knowing her own mother doesn't give a shit about her."

"Good thinking. So how many hours have we gotta sit through then?"

———

"HERE HE IS, the man of the moment. How was your big date last night, Maxi-boy?"

Jimmy, Max's work colleague, flashed a broad white smile as Max trudged into the coffee shop. His smile faded when he saw the state Max was in. "Blimey mate, what did she do to you?"

"I don't wanna talk about it, mate." Max lowered his head as he brushed past Jimmy's six foot muscular frame and hung his coat up behind the counter, wincing as he did so.

"Mate, you don't look right."

"Drop it, will you," Max barked back. He tried to tie his apron around his waist but the pain in his chest made him twitch. Jimmy edged closer.

"What's up, mate? You don't seem yourself. Come on, how long have we known each other, eh?" Jimmy's kind blue eyes convinced Max to soften. Sighing, he led Jimmy into the back room and lifted his shirt. Jimmy looked at Max's scratched and blotchy red skin, stunned into silence. "Jesus, mate, that's a right mess. What's happened?"

"I don't know what got into her last night. Yeah, the sex was wild, but she was…was a nutter, mate. She wouldn't stop."

"That ain't right, that," Jimmy said, pointing at the marks.

"I don't care what she's going through with her mother being missing, that ain't right what she's done to you. Please tell me you've ended it with her?"

Max looked at his shoes. "Well…I just wanted to get out of there, Jim. I wasn't about to break up with a woman holding a knife now, was I?"

Jimmy recoiled. "She did that with a *knife?* A fucking knife. She *is* a bloody nutter." His expression turned more serious. "Text her. Now. Tell her it's over, mate. Fuck me, next time you may not be so lucky."

Max sighed and took his phone out of his back pocket, wincing again as he twisted, then typed out the message.

―――

"Anything?" Hargreaves asked as she poked her head around the door of the CCTV viewing room. Both Rachel and Michelle turned around and shook their heads.

"Nope. Nothing," Rachel answered. "Every camera angle we look at seems to be obscured by a bush or a parked car. The Walkers' driveway is only half visible."

Hargreaves heard the frustrated tone in Rachel's voice. "Right then. Over to Amanda's house. I want that footage from her doorbell camera, and the one on the partition fence, so knock up the neighbour too, Michelle."

"Yes, ma'am," Rachel and Michelle replied in unison, then grabbed their jackets and headed over to the Walker residence.

Going there without a warrant was a bit of a gamble. If Amanda refused to hand the CCTV over and shut the door in her face, Rachel would have no power to force entry in order to seize it, and by the time she came back with a warrant Amanda would have had plenty of time to dispose of it. Rachel had seriously considered applying to the court for a search warrant under Section 8 of PACE, but deep down she was worried that the grounds she currently had, her copper's instinct being the biggest one, might not be strong enough and that the application would be refused. Besides, as long as Amanda invited her in, if she really had to she could seize the CCTV under section 19 of PACE, which gave an officer, lawfully on the premises, the power to seize any property within it, if they had reasonable grounds it was evidence of an offence, without a warrant. Rachel didn't think it would come to that. She was starting to get a feel for Amanda Walker, and she was confident that she would be able to talk her into surrendering the footage voluntarily.

———

AMANDA'S PHONE had beeped ten minutes ago. She lifted a heavy arm from her pillow and rolled over to finally check who it was.

"Over? Fucking prick," she growled after reading Max's message. Before she could text her reply, the doorbell rang. "Fuck's sake."

Throwing on her jumper and jeans, she went downstairs and opened her front door.

"Hello Amanda," Rachel said. She took in Amanda's dishevelled appearance. "Is this a bad time?"

"No it's fine," Amanda replied, yawning. "What's up?"

Rachel looked at the doorbell. "I'd like to check your CCTV footage if I may?"

Amanda froze. "Why? Mum's said she's OK."

"To see if we can establish when your mother left, what state she was in, if anyone was around. The usual sort of thing. When PC Barlow spoke to Poppy the other day, she mentioned that your mother didn't quite seem herself in that message. So, if she wandered off on foot or whatever, maybe this will show that and we can keep the search going for her, as a welfare concern. I'm sure you'd want that?"

Amanda didn't reply, just flashed a watery smile.

"We've checked the local cameras, nothing on those, but it was only the other day that it occurred to me that this," she pointed at the doorbell, "was a camera too. Modern technology, eh."

"I don't know where the footage would be. My mother had it installed, so I guess the app would be on her phone?" Amanda ran a fingernail over a spot of chipped paint on the doorframe.

"I rang the company. They said it was installed on your phone too," Michelle said, quick as a flash. "Can we check your phone?"

Amanda's expression changed. "You want to check my phone?"

"Yes. If that would be OK? Or is there a problem?" Rachel asked.

"But if she wants to be alone that's her right…right?" Amanda replied.

"Of course, she's an adult, but I wouldn't be doing my job properly if I didn't check on her welfare when I think she may not be in the best frame of mind. If I can track her down and she tells me she's fine then we'll leave her, and you, to get on with your lives. I'm sure you've had enough of us by now, right?" Rachel flashed a wry smile.

"I thought that she said that in the message, that she wanted to be left alone."

"Please indulge me here. We all want what's best for your mum."

Amanda paused for a moment and then smiled. "You know what? I do remember a guy came around to install that doorbell. We do have an app, but they also put it on the computer in the office upstairs." Amanda laughed. "But I'm such a technophobe, I couldn't even tell you how it works."

Rachel stepped forward. "Oh, don't you worry about that. PC Barlow here is a techno whizz. May we come in?"

Amanda stepped aside. The three of them went upstairs. Rachel made her way over to the nearest open door.

"No, not in there," Amanda said, with a touch more sharpness in her tone. "In here." She pointed to a door on the opposite side of the landing.

"Oh, sorry," Rachel said, entering the office. "Right, Michelle. Get to work."

"I'll be back in a moment," Amanda said, sidling out of the office and into her bedroom.

———

MICHELLE SAT herself at the office desk and began trawling through the camera footage files. When she found the correct date, she plugged in a USB stick and downloaded it.

"Amanda seems a little twitchy, don't you think?" Rachel said, looking around the door at the landing. "I might have a little mooch around while I'm here."

"That copper's nose again?" Michelle replied.

"Yeah." Rachel headed back onto the landing and noticed Amanda's bedroom door now closed. Inside, she heard a toilet flush. Seconds later the door opened. Amanda recoiled, coming almost nose-to-nose with Rachel.

"Everything OK?" Rachel asked, looking over Amanda's shoulder into her bedroom.

"Yes. Fine," Amanda replied, wiping away a bead of sweat from her brow. She fidgeted in the doorway, trying to obscure Rachel's view. "Did you find what you were looking for?"

"Yes, I think so. PC Barlow has downloaded onto a stick the files leading up to the day your mother disappeared, if that's OK with you?"

Amanda nodded. "I guess so. If you think it will help. Although by now Mother is probably sipping cocktails on a beach somewhere, without even a thought for her worried daughter."

"Without touching her bank account since she was reported missing? I doubt that."

"She may have a stash of money with her. She always did know how to survive."

"Maybe. But let's be sure, eh? Better that than be sorry we missed something. We'll see ourselves out. Thanks again."

―――

AFTER WATCHING Rachel and Michelle descend the stairs, Amanda looked back over her shoulder, relieved that Rachel hadn't looked across the room behind her to the linen basket, where last night's bloodied sheets were now poking out of the part-closed lid. Amanda, relief melting into frustration, walked over to her mother's bedroom and swept her arms across the surface of her dressing table in rage that was now boiling inside of her. She ripped a pillow off the bed and punched it repeatedly.

"That fucking COPPER!" she raged.

―――

"YOU DON'T LIKE HER, do you?" Michelle asked with a mischievous grin.

Rachel looked over at her, then back at the road. "No… It's just something I can't put my finger on." She flicked on her indicator and turned into the police station car park. "A few weeks ago she was adamant that her mother had been kidnapped, or worse. Then we find out she's left of her own volition, to get away from everything, and Amanda, no doubt. And now Amanda seems to be quite bitter about it all. Saying her mother's probably on a beach somewhere living the good life."

Michelle nodded. "Yeah, I've thought from the start her emotions have been all over the place. Probably 'cos she's an only child. Brought up in a broken home, perhaps could be a reason for her behaviour? I mean, this case hasn't been the most straightforward, has it?"

"No, you're right. Let's go and check this footage. See if it sheds any more light on what the hell happened to Diana Walker."

―――

THREE HOURS into the mind-numbingly boring CCTV viewing, Michelle blew her cheeks out and stood up.

"I need caffeine. Usual?"

"Cheers," Rachel replied, running her palm over her eyes.

As Michelle clicked the door shut, Rachel took out her phone and began flicking through her Facebook feed. Then Instagram, then finally Twitter. Every time she looked at a photograph of either her with Adam, or her and her mother, her sighs fluttered out of her, more pained than the last.

"I need to sort this shit," she murmured to the latest photo of her and Adam sat on the white sandy beach in Penzance looking out on the turquoise ocean. Their smiling faces belied the emotion of the day when Adam had told Rachel he'd had enough and was leaving her. The pain of hearing his words in her memory sliced through her heart again.

Rachel had a thought. She typed 'Amanda Walker' into the search bar at the top of her Facebook page. Finding the correct one, she opened up the page to see Amanda's latest exploits. The first picture she saw made her narrow her eyes.

"Here you go," Michelle announced, placing a black coffee in front of Rachel, who was completely transfixed by what was on her screen.

"What do you make of this? Amanda's Facebook page is set to public, not private," Rachel said, passing the phone to Michelle.

"Blimey. Good looking fella. Looks a bit like Zac Efron, I think. That must be Amanda's boyfriend then?"

"I think I've already worked that one out, Shell. He's lying in her bed."

"*Sexy Mofo*," Michelle said, reading out the photo's caption. "Can't argue with that. But why would Amanda be posting something like this when…"

"Exactly. Her dear mother has up sticks and left her, making everyone think she's come to harm, putting Amanda through all that worry, and now she's having wild passionate nights with some fit bloke. This is what I've been saying. It just doesn't fit. For example, I checked Poppy's feeds too, and all she posts are pictures of Diana Walker's missing poster. It's almost as if it was *her* mother that had gone missing."

"Yeah, she's pretty cold. Hey, this hunk works in the Costa in town. He's written it in his profile bio, see?" Michelle pointed at the phone screen then looked down at their mugs. "Fancy a proper coffee?"

———

"You OK, mate?" Jimmy asked across the counter. Max was rubbing a cloth unenthusiastically over one of the coffee machine spouts. Jimmy put down his sandwich. "She texted back yet?"

"Hmm? Oh, no."

"She took it well then. I had her wrong. Least you're not getting earache from her. So, why is your face tripping you?"

"Mum texted me before. Buster's gone missing."

Jimmy stopped chewing and sighed. "Ah, mate, what? How did he get out?"

"Mum said she was sure she'd closed the gate properly, but it must have been open a bit."

"I'm sure he'll turn up. You wanna get an early finish and go look for him? I'll cover."

"Thanks, mate. I might just do that." As Max lifted his apron over his head he winced again.

"And get some Savlon on those cuts as well," Jimmy said as he walked into the back to bin his sandwich wrapper.

Max turned to grab his coat.

"Excuse me, could we have two lattes and five minutes of your time, please?" Rachel said, appearing at the counter.

"Sorry, didn't hear you come in. Lattes, was it?"

"Yeah. You mind if I ask you a few questions?"

"About what?" Max asked as he got their order ready.

"Hey, I recognise you. You're investigating the Walker case."

"Correct," Rachel replied, taking out her warrant card. "Detective Inspector Rachel Morrison. This here is PC Barlow. I wanted to ask you about Amanda. You *are* her boyfriend, right?"

"Not anymore." Max looked down at the counter and fiddled with a teaspoon.

Rachel fought the look of intrigue that crossed her face. "Oh, right. How come?"

"Why are you asking?" Max countered.

"Well, I'm sure she's told you, but we've had word from her mother that she's safe and well so we're closing the case. We just wanted to make sure Amanda had a network of support around her, seeing as though her mother has left her unexpectedly." Max remained silent. "So, who called it off?" Rachel probed.

"I did," Max replied. Rachel waited a moment before prompting him to continue, which he did somewhat reluctantly. "She's been acting really weird recently. Not returning my calls, being off the grid. I figured it was because she was worried about her mum being missing. But now you tell me her mother is safe, it makes what happened last night even more weird."

"What happened last night?" Rachel asked, thinking back to the photo on Facebook she'd seen that morning.

Max blushed. "Well, it's a little embarrassing actually."

"Trust me, I'm unshockable. Just ask Michelle." Rachel

141

turned and nodded to Michelle who waved back, just as her phone rang.

"Back in a minute," Michelle said, stepping outside.

"Come and sit with me here in the corner. It's quiet," Rachel said, leading Max to the corner furthest away from anybody else in the café. "Tell me what happened."

Max sat down and sighed. "I saw a completely different side to Amanda. It was like… Like…" He shook his head as he recalled the wild but frightening night he'd shared with Amanda.

"Like?" Rachel encouraged.

"She went crazy on me. I went round there. She'd texted me earlier in the day, but then called me when she knew I'd finished my shift. Sounded in a bit of a state so I went to the off license on the way and picked up a bottle of wine. Wasn't the best type, but I don't get paid until the end of the week, so I did my best." He looked down, embarrassed. "Anyway, she'd been avoiding me for a few days. I just thought it was 'cos she had a lot on with the police and the press sniffing around. So I gave her her space. I sent flowers though, and cards. Got most of my updates through Poppy on Instagram. But then last night Amanda called me. I went round and all she seemed interested in was fucking. Now, I'm not against that, but she was different last night. Really weird. She tied me to the bed using handcuffs, blindfolded me and then…" Max paused and swallowed.

"What happened to you, Max?"

"She took out a knife. A fucking massive knife. She cut me. Quite deep." He lifted his t-shirt. His wounds were still scarlet, two of the deeper ones still weeping. "And then she got on top and fucked me. I kept saying to stop but she didn't. She wanted me to see I was bleeding, and seemed to enjoy watching me squirm, you know? Proper fucked up stuff. Then I thought, does that seem like somebody who's worried sick about her mum being missing?"

Michelle came hurrying back into the café, phone in hand.

"Boss, that was Poppy. She said Diana Walker has just called her."

Both Rachel and Max's eyebrows raised.

"What did she say?"

"She told Poppy she's by the sea. Said she'd had enough and wanted to end it all."

"Shit. Did Poppy ask her where exactly she was?"

"No, but we have Diana's phone number from when she last called in. As soon as I got off the phone with Poppy, I called tech and asked them to run a check on which mast the signal bounced off. By the time we get back to the station they should have it."

"Great work, Michelle. We need to get to her." Rachel turned to Max, who looked as confused as ever. "Thank you, Max, for your time."

He shrugged. "No problem."

She reached into her pocket and gave him her card. "Max, I suspect that, deep down, you know that what Amanda did to you was very wrong and that it amounts to both a serious sexual assault and grievous bodily harm. No one should be made to go through an experience like that, and I want you to seriously consider making a statement about what happened. I know it won't be easy, but if you choose to do so, you will be supported by us through the entire process." Seeing the reluctance on his face, she added, "I want you to think about it overnight and call me tomorrow so that we can discuss the matter in greater detail because no one should be allowed to do that to another human being."

He nodded. "I'll think about it."

"I want you to go to your GP and get the injuries looked at and documented," she said. "Also, take some photos of them tonight. Get someone else to do it if you can. If you decide you want to take this further after we speak, I'll arrange for a police photographer to take formal record photography, but the selfies will be a good start. Call me in the morning, OK?"

She could see the embarrassment in his eyes and knew

that he wouldn't call but at least she had tried. She found Michelle waiting for her outside. "You get back to the station, Michelle. I'll grab a cab from here."

"Where are you going now, boss?" Michelle asked as they closed the café door behind them.

"Where do you think?"

Chapter 17

"Hello, Poppy. Can I come in?"

"Of course. PC Barlow passed on my message then?" Poppy replied as she opened her front door for Rachel to pass through into the narrow hallway.

"Yes. As it happens, I received a call from her just a minute ago. We managed to get the signal off Diana's phone coming from Prussia Cove. It's near Penzance. Does that mean anything to you?" They walked into the kitchen. Like Amanda's, it had been pristinely cleaned and organised by Poppy, but the brass and mahogany fixtures and fittings were much more dated.

"Wow, actually yes, it does. Amanda told me they used to holiday there when she was younger. That was part of the reason why they moved here after her father passed away. It's a private estate, but they had friends there, so it was a nice little bolthole for them to get away to. That place meant a lot to them both. I'm not surprised Diana felt at home there. Especially in her fragile state of mind. I hope she doesn't go through with what she was saying." Poppy paused to wipe her nose on a tissue.

"Do you know where Amanda is? I went round to her house before I came here, but there was no one home."

"I don't know. I'm going over there later though. I've made a casserole. I don't think she's looking after herself since her mother left."

"Tell me about Amanda, Poppy." Rachel sat down at the kitchen counter.

"What do you want to know?"

"Everything," Rachel replied.

———

It was almost 6 p.m. by the time Rachel finally left Poppy's house, a lot more informed about Amanda than when she'd entered. Deciding to try the Walker residence again, she turned off the highway and headed straight there.

"Detective inspector, hi," Amanda said when she opened her front door. Rachel noticed her face looked flushed and the tips of her beige suede boots were still wet.

"Hello Amanda. I called round earlier, but you were out. Been anywhere nice?" Rachel's tones were clipped, but Amanda was too preoccupied with sweeping up a couple of leaves that had blown down her hallway.

"Just out for a walk. Clear my head, you know?"

"Have you spoken to Poppy today?"

"No, why? She's coming over later. Again. I swear that girl thinks I can't even fry an egg."

"Must be nice though, to have such a caring friend?"

"I guess."

Amanda led the way into the kitchen, all the while looking down at her phone and typing out a message. Rachel looked over her shoulder as she walked and noticed a half-written Facebook message to Max. Playing dumb, Rachel smiled.

"Boyfriend?"

Amanda looked up from her phone. "Yeah. Well, kind of. His dog went missing this morning. He was posting to ask everybody to keep an eye out, so I shared it on my page. I was just checking in to see if there was any news."

"That's kind of you. Listen, I need to tell you something about your mother. Poppy received a call from her earlier on today, and to be completely honest with you, Amanda, we're very concerned about your mother's state of mind, with what she said in her phone call to Poppy. We traced the signal and located your mother at a place called Prussia Cove near Penzance. Poppy told me you used to visit there on holiday when you were younger?"

"Yes, we did. I used to love leaning into the wind up on the cliffs, pretending my coat was Superman's cape." Amanda's eyes misted over for a second, before refocussing with more urgency. "What are you guys gonna do now? About Mum? You gonna go check on her? You make it sound like she's gonna throw herself off those cliffs or something. She could have already done it by now, with you lot wasting time."

It wasn't the tone of Amanda's voice that surprised Rachel, it was the specifics in her words. "We have alerted the local police; they are looking for her around that location. I thought you would now want to make your own way over there yourself, now you know where she is."

Remembering Max's story, and the two different Amandas they'd both experienced, Rachel held her stare on Amanda for a moment too long until she began explaining herself.

"Yeah, I should do. But I've been so upset lately, and I'm not sleeping, so I don't think it's safe to drive just now. I'll wait until Poppy finishes work tomorrow, then maybe she could take me over?"

Their eyes locked as they sussed each other out. Rachel's phone then rang, making them both jump.

"Hi Michelle, you—."

"You need to get back to the office. *Now.*"

———

"Right, show me what you've got," Rachel said as she strode into the CCTV room, throwing her jacket on the back of her chair.

"When I went through this last file, I saw something that you're going to find *very* interesting. Look." Michelle clicked the mouse on the play button.

Clear to see, Amanda was crouching behind her mother's BMW. She then stood up and began running an object along the side of the car, leaving a deep scratch, all the way through the blue paint to the grey metal.

"It was on the morning her mother disappeared. Right before she went to the garage. What a cow," Michelle said.

"Lying bitch!" Rachel exclaimed. "She put that mechanic through the mill of suspicion, causing his partner to lose the baby, and it was her all along. We're in the shit for this one. Why didn't we check this sooner?"

"We didn't know we had it. These doorbell camera thingies are pretty new and when I asked about CCTV, Amanda played the idiot, remember?" Michelle said. "Also, while you were out, I wanted to know what Amanda's been up to lately, and the signal on *her* phone showed she had been up at Lizard Point a few times. Nothing suspicious there, maybe she went for a walk to clear her head, you may be thinking? But Amanda isn't the rough and ready, rugged type, is she? She prefers nightclubs and parties, if her Instagram feed is anything to go by."

Rachel smiled. "You have been busy, haven't you? Go on."

"Well, the only known feature up there at Lizard Point is a friggin' lighthouse. Apart from the Anchor Pub, that is, but that's a half mile walk away back down the coastal path, and not the sort of place a rich woman like Amanda would frequent. So, why is it only since her mother disappeared that she's been there? Her phone never pinged the mast near there before, so why now? Something sinister is going on," Michelle said, shaking her head.

"She's a piece of work alright. From what Max alluded to

when I spoke to him earlier, it sounds like she not only GBHed him last night, but she also committed a serious sexual assault as part of a sex game that he didn't want. She's messed up for sure."

"Does he want to make a complaint against her for that?" Michelle asked, sensing an opportunity to bring Amanda in.

"I've told him he should, but I can't see it happening. I also told him to go to his GP in the morning."

"She needs a therapist, that's what I think."

"She was seeing one, remember?" Rachel said. "See if you can find out who it was and let me know where they live. I think I need to have a meeting with them to see if we can find out what they covered in their sessions."

"Won't he just claim patient-client privilege?'

"Oh, I'm sure he'll know his legal rights, and stake his claim to them, but it's worth a shot. Who knows? He might feel he's obligated to talk. If not, we can always apply for a production order from the Crown Court to force him to comply, although getting one would be a real ball-ache. Can't hurt putting the pressure on him. Anyway, great work again, Michelle, but keep searching through that CCTV when it comes back from Prussia Cove. We need more than the keying of a car to build a case against her. But at least it proves she is a liar. And it makes finding Diana Walker even more important. I'll go see what I can find at the lighthouse."

STEPPING out of her car at the top of the muddy dirt track along the most accessible end of the coastal path, Rachel pulled her coat tighter around herself, the chill of the southwest wind biting deep. The whitewashed lighthouse was the dominating presence on an otherwise featureless landscape. She walked along the thin track, the crashing waves far below her reminding her to be extra careful not to go to near the cliff edge, especially as the light was fading.

"Can I 'elp you?" a gruff voice, with a broad Cornish accent, sounded just as Rachel pushed on the lighthouse door. Startled, she spun round. There stood over her was a very tall, thickset, middle-aged man, with a straggly grizzled beard. His deeply lined face was weatherbeaten and he was wearing a navy blue fisherman's smock, yellow waterproof jacket and cargo trousers. On his head was a black wool hat.

"Oh, sorry. Do you live here?"

"Why?" he snapped.

Rachel fished out her warrant card. "Do you live here?" she repeated.

The fisherman glanced at the warrant card momentarily, then glared again at Rachel. "I do, why?"

"Have you seen a blue BMW car here at all this week?"

The fisherman set his lips. "Nope," he mumbled. He reached into his jacket and took out a long piece of blue twine with a key attached.

"Do you recognise this girl?" Rachel took out her phone and pinched the screen on a Facebook photo of Amanda.

"Nope," he replied, barely looking at the photo. He turned the key in the lock and stepped inside the lighthouse.

Rachel searched for another photo. "How about this woman? Do you recognise her?" She showed him a photo of Diana Walker.

"Nope." Before he could push the door closed in her face, Rachel stuck out an arm.

"OK," she said, her palm flat against the weathered oak door. "Can I ask you to call me if you do see these women, or the car?" She handed him her card. "Call me right away, OK?"

The fisherman snatched the card and grunted.

"Thanks."

Rachel turned and headed back to her car, as the fisherman pushed the door closed and locked it from the inside. Before she reached where she had parked her car, she saw a lone figure on the edge of the cliff looking out to sea. Fearing the worst, Rachel strode over there.

"Hey, you there. Can you come back from the edge, please?"

The figure turned around. He was around sixty years old, with a shock of white hair blowing in the stiff breeze. He wore dirty blue jeans, a dark grey ribbed knit jumper and a jacket way too thin to be keeping him warm in the biting coastal wind. Rachel recognised him immediately as Dave from the Anchor Pub. Guessing that he had probably had a skinful by this time, as usual, Rachel hurried over to him and clasped his arm. "Dave? It's Rachel. Are you OK?"

Dave looked back at her through watery, red eyes. "The lights usually come from o'er there. See?" he mumbled, pointing to a part of the Lizard Point headland as far as the eye could see. "They're there and then they aren't. Like whate'er is makin' them jus' disappears like magic."

"These lights, Dave. Can you describe them? What colour are they? White, yellow, red, green? Could it be a low flying plane? Or a boat?"

"No boat dare sail round that headland. Not wi' those rocks," Dave replied in his thick Cornish accent. "Lived here all my life, and ne'er once known a fishing boat to attempt it. It's notorious that spot. Even ol' Al Gregory o'er there in that lighthouse wouldn't go around there. 'Suicide to do that', he allus says." Dave paused to take a drink from his hip flask then wiped a hand over his grey stubble.

"Let me drop you home, Dave. Pearl will be worried about you." Rachel guided him away from the edge and over to her car.

"Steak and kidney pie for tea tonight, Pearl said."

"Ooh, lovely. That wife of yours is a good one, eh, Dave?"

"Mmm," Dave replied, taking one last look out to sea. "Will you look into what's makin' those lights, Rachel? I got a feelin' it's somethin' important."

"Will do, Dave. Now, let's get you home to Pearl and your pie, shall we?"

―――

Taking another look at Rachel's card, the fisherman walked over to his phone and picked up the handset. He tapped his fingers on the table as he waited for the line to connect.

"Why do I have the pissin' police crawlin' all over my property, askin' if I've seen the girl whose mum has gone missin'?" he barked down the line.

Chapter 18

"So, how did you get on last night?" Michelle asked as Rachel sat down at her desk and sipped her morning coffee.

"Well, I spoke to the fisherman who seems to live there. He said he hasn't seen anyone who matches the description of Amanda, or her mother, or Amanda's car. How about you?"

"I've been doing some digging, and found out that Amanda was having therapy with a man called Richard Baker. He has his own private practice at his home in St. Ruan."

"OK. So at least we have a name now."

"Don't you recognise that name?" Michelle then realised why. "Oh, of course, you hadn't moved here back then, had you? Well, he was the guy whose daughter got murdered. Quite horrifically, as it goes. I felt sorry for the poor sod. He does a lot for the community now, to turn his grief into a positive."

"What case was that?" Rachel asked, sitting up straight.

"His daughter's killers burned her alive. Some out of town detectives offered to work on the case out of hours as it was so grotesque, but the scumbag killer got a shit sentence because of her age, and there was some kind of technicality."

"*Her?*" Rachel asked.

"I know," Michelle replied, nodding.

"Wow. You don't hear of that very often. Fucking hell. It sounds like *he* needs the therapy. That's gonna fuck you up no matter who you are."

"I don't know how he managed to cope with it. I'd be one angry bitch. I wonder how he dealt with it?"

Rachel checked her watch. "I think I'll go over there now, ask him a few general questions about Amanda. Did anything come back from the coppers we sent over to Prussia Cove?"

"Nothing. They showed the locals Diana's photo, but no one remembers seeing her."

"Right. OK." Rachel rose from her desk, a determined look on her face. "Well, we need to crack on. If Diana Walker is in some kind of trouble, personal or otherwise, we need to start getting some tangible leads. Hargreaves is getting twitchy again."

"Press are sniffing around. They've got wind we're still investigating her as a misper."

"Well, we are, I guess. Until I see Diana Walker alive and well in front of me, we keep looking." Rachel pushed her chair underneath her desk and picked up her handbag.

"Roger that. See you later," Michelle said, returning to her paperwork.

———

"RICHARD BAKER?" Rachel asked, as the smart, black door to a very expensive red brick mansion opened. Behind the door stood a dark-haired, middle-aged man wearing dark blue denim jeans and a purple Ralph Lauren shirt.

"Yes," the man replied. "And you are?"

Rachel fished into her pocket and took out her warrant card. "Detective Inspector Rachel Morrison. May I have five minutes of your time?"

Baker leaned in and strained his eyes through his expensive looking frameless glasses to look at Rachel's ID. "What's this in relation to?"

"A local lady, Diana Walker, has been missing for over a couple of weeks now. There have been no sightings of her and no activity on her phone or credit cards. So, we're just making some routine enquiries, talking to people who knew the family, that sort of thing."

"I see. Please, come in."

He stood away from the door and allowed Rachel to pass into the opulent hallway. The walls were laden with expensive looking artwork and dominating the hallway was a huge staircase leading up to a gallery landing.

"You have a beautiful home, Dr. Baker. And your therapy business is based here too?"

"Yes. Yes, it is. I have an office in the extension at the back." He folded his arms. "So, how can I help you with your enquiries, inspector?"

"One of your clients, Amanda Walker, is the daughter of our missing woman. I was hoping you could give me a bit of an insight as to what Amanda was coming to therapy for?"

Baker let out a derisory snort. "Inspector, you know I can't divulge private information about my patients."

Rachel smiled. "So, she *is* one of your patients? And yes, I know that I can't force you to talk about your patients. However, I am sure you know that I could go to a judge and get him to force you to cooperate. That can be a lengthy and, well, intrusive process, which I am sure we both want to avoid. So, if you have nothing to hide I think it is in both of our interests for you to answer my questions and for me to leave you in peace."

Baker's left eye twitched. He paused a moment, scratching his chin. "As I said, I can't talk about the specifics but I sense you may already know the answer to some of the questions you are asking. So, let's chat and see where it takes us." He turned his back. "Would you like a drink? Coffee, tea?"

He led her into the pristine kitchen, complete with black high gloss worktops and expensive Neff appliances.

"Oh, no thank you. I won't put you to any trouble, I know

it's early. I have reason to believe Amanda may be involved in a serious crime, so if I may ask you some questions about her, it would be very helpful to our case."

"Serious crime? What is it she's supposedly done?"

Rachel paused, realising she didn't actually have a definitive answer to that question. Going with the one thing she did have hard evidence of, she straightened her back. "She has been caught on camera causing criminal damage to her mother's car. Quite significant damage."

Baker gave a slight smile. "Oh dear."

"So, you can see why we would like to gather some more intel on Amanda's state of mind, given that her mother has now gone missing. Has Amanda ever mentioned harming her mother in any way, in any of her sessions?"

Baker thought for a moment, then shook his head. "Look, you know I can't talk about my patients. You've already worked out she was my patient, so that's no secret. However, I can't put anything on record. It would ruin my reputation. However, off the record…" He paused and looked Rachel in the eyes. "Off the record, I don't have any recollection of her saying she would harm her mother."

"Has she ever said anything in your sessions that you would perceive as concerning?"

"I'd have to say no on that one too. She's just working through some things in her past. Pretty standard entry requirements for seeking therapy really."

"I assume you keep client notes from your sessions?"

Baker's smile faded. "Yes, I do. For reference so I know where to pick up with them next time."

"I'd like a copy of Amanda's notes, please. Redacted in places, if they must be. But your cooperation with anything you can help us with would be very much appreciated, Dr. Baker."

———

The icy-cold wind howled as it blew across Lizard Point, bending over every shrub and fern it buffeted against. The white peaks of the waves below rolled over and crashed against the sharp rocks, smothering them with freezing ocean water.

"Where the fuck have you been? You said six." A tall, athletic looking man seethed as The Therapist approached him standing at the foot of the lighthouse. He pulled his Thinsulate woolly hat down over his ears and held the collar of his wool coat close to his neck. He was in his early thirties with piercing blue eyes and a light brown stubble beard. "The Fisherman has filled me in on this shitstorm that's going down here. He's gone up already." He nodded to the top of the lighthouse.

"Sorry, couldn't get out. The wife was faffing about. Had one of your lot visit me this afternoon. Know anything about that?" The Therapist squinted into the biting southwesterly wind.

The man shrugged his broad shoulders and ran a hand over his chiselled jaw, smoothing down his stubble. "Nothing to do with me. I don't work in that station. Why would I want any attention coming our way? It's bad enough being caught up in this shit for how long now?"

The Therapist scowled. "Stop whining. You knew the job when you volunteered."

"Whining? This has gone way too far, Rich. You told me this was all finished, after the last one. Three you said. That was it." He jabbed his finger into The Therapist's face.

"Keep a lid on it, will you!" The Therapist barked, swatting the man's gloved finger away. "And remember, we don't use names, only aliases here. None of that 'Rich' crap. I'm The Therapist and you're The Copper, you got that?"

"It's such a load of bollocks, all this," The Copper growled. He paced the marshy ground outside the lighthouse, stopping to cast his gaze out to sea. "My role in all of this was simple. I texted Amanda the info on the target from a burner phone. I set up the scene, and then she comes in and does the business. I clear up the mess, bring them to The Fisherman and he sorts out the rest from there. They go down as just another missing person and the police file it as another case their budget cuts won't allow them to get round to." He turned and pressed his face into The Therapist's. "So how the *fuck* did this mess happen?"

"Amanda's gone rogue. She wants to kill her mother."

The Copper recoiled. "You what?"

"Yeah. Her mum's currently locked up somewhere. Sick or what?"

"Fucking hell. What does Amanda want from us?"

The Therapist let out a long breath. "She's concocted this story to the police over the last few weeks, making out she's been kidnapped. Her mother will then mysteriously, and conveniently, make a call from the edge of these cliffs or something. Then…well, you can imagine the rest." He pointed over the edge into darkness.

"Why?"

"So, when her mother's call is listened to, Amanda can blame the police for doing a shitty job investigating her mother's disappearance. She wants to sue them for being negligent, with her mother being vulnerable. She's making it look like suicide. Then the press will blame the police, and Amanda will literally get away with murder."

"What does she want from us if she's got it all planned out?"

The Therapist's frustration was growing by the second. "Come on, for fuck's sake, you're a copper. What's the one part of our *procedure* that Amanda's not involved in?"

The Copper thought for a moment, then looked out to sea. "Disposing of the body. Cleaning up the scene."

"She wants us to do that for her. To get rid of her mother's body. Otherwise she'll expose the whole bloody lot of us. The others are on their way here to discuss what we do."

The Fisherman wrenched open the door of the lighthouse, his face like thunder. "Right, come in then. Everythin's prepared."

The Copper, still reeling from the Therapist's revelation, stood back. "Amanda can fuck off. No. This ain't like any of the other jobs. This is murder for murder's sake. Her mother hasn't done anything wrong like those other bastards." He turned to walk back to his car. "I'm done with all that shit now. I don't need the money that bad to get in the shit with this. It all died down and nobody went looking for those other three people. We all got away with it. And they were the scum of the earth. So it's justice. *This* is wrong."

The Therapist let out a long sigh of defeat. "The problem is, Amanda has an audio recording of all our involvement in the three murders."

The Copper turned around. "You what?" he said, horrified.

"She said that if we don't get rid of her mother in the way we have done the other three, she will kill her anyway and no doubt make a hatchet job of getting rid of her body. And when she gets caught, she'll take us all down with her." He walked over to The Copper. "So, we either help her commit one murder, and get away with it, or we all get done for four murders."

"Hobson's bloody choice then, isn't it?" The Copper said, pocketing his car keys. "But I'm warning you. As soon as you deviate from how it's worked before, things always go wrong. People make mistakes. We could all get caught anyway. Then we are all fucked. For nothing. And an innocent woman would be dead."

As they stood in the moonlight, The Teacher, The Nurse and The Gardener approached the lighthouse from the coastal path, looking windblown and frozen to the bone.

"Who's he?" The Nurse asked the Therapist, as she looked at The Copper.

"Part of the organisation. You just haven't met him before."

"Come inside. All of you," The Fisherman barked. "Even this meetin' is a poxy risk if we get seen."

"Amanda just wants to know where the burying place is. I have to tell her. What else can I do? It'll save us all," The Therapist said as he descended the steps to their usual meeting room, following the others.

The Fisherman, walking behind him, stopped dead on the top step.

"*You* know where it is?" The Copper exclaimed, looking up at him from the step below. "I thought only he was supposed to know?" He pointed up to The Fisherman.

The Therapist stared down at The Copper. "Of course I know. All of this was my idea, remember? I asked The Fisherman where would be a good place to bury the bitch who murdered my daughter, when she came out of prison. I wanted to make sure it was the darkest depth of hell imaginable. Luckily, he knew just the spot. Then I heard about all the other worthless bastards in this area who deserved the same punishment and I had to do something."

"It became a bit of a habit though, didn't it?" The Fisherman said. "I didn't plan on doin' it three times more for you."

"We were doing good work. That damn Amanda. Why did she have to ruin this?" The Therapist's normal, cool exterior slipped for a second. He smoothed his hair back and set himself.

"You know what? Fuck it. Tell 'er. Tell this Amanda where the bodies are, who gives a fuck. Let 'er dump 'er mum 'erself though, that's my compromise." The Fisherman jabbed a finger at the Therapist as they all walked into the meeting room. "Not a single sailor dare go out around that headland, I've made sure o' that, after the horror stories I've spread around this village about that current, and those bastard rocks. No one even knows *I* go out there, I'm so careful not to be seen by anyone. I pick my time perfectly. Tell you what, I'll even tell 'er how to weigh the body down correctly." The Fisherman banged his fist against the table. "But I will *not* let 'er use my fuckin' boat."

"Where is it?" The Nurse asked in a quiet voice. The others turned to face her.

"What?" The Therapist replied.

"The burying place."

The Fisherman let out a grumpy sigh. "Mullion Cove. In a part where no one e'er goes. There's a point where the seabed is at its deepest. I weigh 'em down, so they sink to the bottom and become fish food. Believe me, no one is findin' them. But I won't be blackmailed by some rich bitch." He turned to face The Therapist. "I don't care about the secret any more, just tell 'er where it is."

"We can't. We're not killers!" The Teacher exclaimed. "Her mum is innocent. How can we sit back with all the torment we already have in our head, and knowingly let this monster kill an innocent person? How long has she been locked up now? A week? Two? More? We can't keep this to ourselves."

"We have to," The Gardener said in a quiet voice. The group turned to stare open-mouthed at him. There was a lengthy pause. "Look, if we don't, we all go to prison for knowing about the other murders. We've all played a part in them. We've got no choice." He sank his face into his hands.

The air in the room was thick with silence. One voice pierced through it. "I've got an idea." The group looked at the speaker. It was The Copper, who had been sitting quietly, thinking methodically throughout the panic.

"We're going about this the wrong way, don't you think? Amanda wants us to make someone disappear for her, and we don't want to do that, right?"

"Right," the group said in unison.

"The answer, it's staring us in the face," The Copper said, smiling.

"Spit it out, man," The Fisherman barked.

"Why don't we just make *Amanda* disappear?" The Copper replied.

Chapter 19

"Hi, I got your message. Chinese, right?"

Poppy held up a takeaway bag as Amanda stood back to let her through her front door. "How are you doing?"

Amanda sighed at length as they walked into the kitchen. "Yeah, I'm doing OK, in the circumstances. I mean, what can I do? If my mum decides to kill herself and leave me alone in the world, then what can I do?"

"Oh, Mand. I'm sure it won't come to that. What did the police say last time they were here?"

"Nothing… But, anyway. It obviously got too much for Max. He dumped me. Seems like everybody is leaving me right now." Amanda took out a box from the takeaway bag and ripped off its plastic lid.

Poppy tutted. "Max dumped you? Of all the times. What an arse."

"I know, I'm better off without." Amanda picked up a fork and began tucking into her chow mein.

Poppy spooned out her fried rice onto a white dinner plate. "Oh, I was meaning to ask. You never did tell me what happened with that dodgy group you were looking into?"

Amanda coughed and wiped her mouth with a piece of kitchen roll. "Oh, nothing. Never found anything. Dead end, really." She put her fork down and fixed a mischievous stare on Poppy. "Hey, what's say we get drunk tonight? You can help me drown my sorrows."

Poppy hesitated. "I'd better not. I've got work in the morning."

Amanda grunted. "Oh, come on, Pops. Don't be a total bore. You're supposed to be here cheering me up."

"Oh, OK. Why not?" Poppy relented. "Shall I get a bottle from the cellar? I know where the good stuff is."

"No," Amanda said, so abruptly it made Poppy jump slightly. "I've got a bottle in the fridge Max brought round the other night. We'll have that."

―――

Poppy raced along the high street, the library just in her sights up ahead. Stopping just outside to catch her breath, she smoothed her hair down and tried to look like she hadn't flopped into bed in Amanda's spare room at 3 a.m. Inside, Margaret was standing behind the returns desk with a queue waiting. Using that as cover, Poppy slung her bag underneath the counter and took the customer behind the one Margaret was serving. As soon as the rush was over, Margaret turned and gave Poppy a withering stare.

"This isn't like you, Poppy. You're never late."

"I know, Margaret, I'm—"

"You've changed. And not for the better," Margaret interjected. "I mean, what's that coat all about? A leather jacket and jeans for work?"

"I know. I'm sorry. I was at Amanda's last night and I spilt some food on my clothes, so she lent me some of hers to wear. I actually think they suit me." Poppy half-twirled, but Margaret was unmoved.

"I need to speak to you about something." Margaret clasped her hands in front of her. "As you know, the council approved the extra funding for another year, so the assistant manager's job has been given the green light. They've asked me who I would recommend to take on the responsibility of this position and…"

Poppy's eyes widened. "Yes?"

"I'm sorry, Poppy, but given your timekeeping lately, and your slip in personal standards, I had no option but to recommend Jill over there." She pointed to a dowdy looking middle-aged woman wearing a grey cardigan and beige flannel trousers. She swept a lock of mousy brown hair out of her heavy-lidded eyes and waved back.

"Jill? She's only a temp. I've been here for years."

"I'm sorry, Poppy." Margaret tapped Poppy's arm, then went back into her office.

"Well, if you're expecting me to give up a friend in need, for a promotion, then you can stuff it," Poppy replied under her breath. The next book she picked up felt the full force of her date stamp.

———

MICHELLE'S HEAD appeared around Rachel's desk partition. "I've just received a call from the police in Prussia Cove. They've found a handbag washed up on the beach. The ID inside says it belongs to Diana Walker."

Rachel almost choked on her coffee. "Shit."

"The location matches up with the area Diana's phone pinged from."

"But no body as yet?"

"No. But they're still looking along the coastline. The temperature of that water, though, and the strong tide. It's not looking good if she has gone in off the end of that pier."

"Pier?" Rachel asked.

"Yeah. There's a long pier that would have been the most likely spot for her to have jumped in. The waves are at their strongest, and her bag was found not far from there."

"Fuck. Right. Get the local plod on door-to-door and get

the CCTV to see if we can see Diana Walker in the vicinity. I need it double quick time, Michelle."

"On it," Michelle replied, grabbing her jacket. On her way out she passed Superintendent Hargreaves walking over to Rachel's desk.

"What's the latest?" Hargreaves asked.

"Well, ma'am. It's unfortunately now pointing towards suicide. But as yet no body has been found."

"Look, Rachel. You've had long enough to solve this case. It's still eating up resources we could be using for more urgent cases. You know the kind of pressure I am under. I've given you a lot of freedom here but I think it's about time you handed it over to the Missing Persons Unit and they can tie up the loose ends if it does come back as suicide." She perched on the end of Rachel's desk and leaned in. "You're too close to this case to let it go, I see that. But it's not a murder case anymore, so I need my best detective back. And you have hardly spent any time at home recently. Your husband's probably forgotten what you look like by now."

Rachel swallowed and bit back the tears at the mention of Adam. "With respect, ma'am, Diana Walker is still a high risk missing person who we have grounds to believe is suicidal. The Missing Persons Unit doesn't have the same resources that I have as head of reactive crime. If we scale down the enquiry, as you suggest, and hand it back to the Misper Unit, the press would have a field day if she turns up dead."

Hargreaves continued undaunted. "I need to give answers to that bloody MP and the press as to what's happening with cases that we haven't had time to start investigating yet. I can't justify anymore why I have my head of reactive CID working on a case that should have been closed days ago. Can you see my point?"

Rachel nodded. "Of course I can. But I just feel there's more to this one. So many loose ends. And Amanda. She has more to do with this, I'm sure of it."

"She probably drove her mum to suicide, knowing what

we know of her. She sounds like a spoiled brat. But we don't always get the ending to cases we expect. You've been in this game long enough to know that. You're looking for something that isn't there. If somebody felt the only way out was suicide, while that's tragic, it's up to them. You have other cases to work on, and I can't justify spending taxpayers' money on a copper's hunch. Leave this one to the Misper Unit."

"Ma'am," Rachel replied. Hargreaves got up from the desk and headed back into her office. In her pocket, Rachel's phone vibrated. "Hi Mum." After a moment or two of hearing her mother's angry voice, Rachel interjected. "Hey, slow down. I'm sorry. What time was the appointment again? I know you wanted me to come with you. No, of course I wouldn't be better off if you croaked it. I don't care about the life insurance money, Mum, that's not funny." Rachel dragged a hand through her hair. "Look, I can still make it in time to take you. No, you don't need to get a cab. Mum. *Mum.*" She kicked out at the leg of the desk in frustration as her mother hung up.

In the silence that followed, something clicked in Rachel's mind. Something her mother had said on the phone. She riffled through the evidence file in her desk drawer and located the list of Amanda's outgoing calls. There it was in black and white.

"Cold bitch," Rachel muttered. She jumped up and strode over to Hargreaves' office.

"Come in."

"Ma'am. I'm sorry to keep raking over the coals of this one, but I knew there was something not quite right about it."

"The Walker case, no doubt," Hargreaves replied, taking off her glasses. "I have just told you to give this case up. Was I not clear?"

"Yes, but…" Rachel held out the call log and pointed at the entry in question.

Hargreaves sighed and took the paper. "What am I looking at here? It better be good."

167

"The day after Diana Walker first called in to us, from the train she was supposed to be on, Amanda made a call to AXA insurance."

"And?" Hargreaves' patience was wearing thin.

"My mother uses them. She's been feeling down lately and wanted to protect me against, well, if she wasn't thinking too clearly one day and did something daft. They insure people for that eventuality. You pay a massive premium for that, though, but she got it anyway."

"I'm not following, Rachel. What eventuality?"

"Suicide, ma'am. Amanda Walker made a call to an insurance company the day *after* her mother rang to say she was safe and well, and thinking of taking a little holiday to recuperate. Don't you think that's strange?"

Before Hargreaves could give her answer, a pair of knuckles rapped on the door.

"Sorry, guv, call for you at your desk. He says it's urgent," the PC announced.

Hargreaves waved Rachel away. "We'll talk about this later."

"Fuck's sake," Rachel muttered under her breath as she excused herself and returned to her desk. "Morrison." She clenched her teeth when the man began to slur his words down the line. "Dave, I haven't got time for this. No, we haven't looked into the lights you've seen out to sea yet. We're very stretched and everything will be looked at in due course. I know you think this is important, but unfortunately there are other pressing issues at hand. Thank you for your call. Goodbye."

———

Rachel bumped into Michelle in the police station corridor by the vending machine.

"We've got a possible new lead," Michelle told her.

"Yeah? Keep it under wraps though for the moment.

Hargreaves is trying to have us pulled away from this case. I think we might be off it by the morning. I've bought a bit more time, so the pressure is on. What is it?"

"Diana Walker's window cleaner has just called me to say he was surprised she still wasn't found. He said he remembered that Amanda and Diana were arguing 'really bad' when he last did her windows."

"Significance?" Rachel asked.

"Amanda said they *never* argued. Remember?"

"COME ON, Richard. We'll be late back if you keep dawdling," Sonia Baker snapped at her husband, who was a few steps behind her and struggling to hold three carrier bags full of groceries.

"I'm doing the best I can here, love," he replied. The handle on one bag snapped, sending apples rolling all over the high street pavement. "Fucking hell." He booted one apple across the road in fury.

"I think you should go for a lie down when we get home. You've not been yourself for a few days now," Sonia said in his ear as he rose after picking up the remaining apples.

Taking her advice, he trudged up the stairs when they returned home and closed the bedroom door behind him. Lying on the bed, he began typing out a message on his phone.

`Fix this situation. You know what I mean.`

His thumb hovered over the send button just as Sonia called up to him.

"Coming, love," he replied, putting his phone back in his pocket.

Slumping down on her couch, Rachel looked longingly at the bottle of wine she'd bought on the way home. Able to resist no longer, she unscrewed the top and poured a large glass and downed it almost in one gulp. Her takeaway remained untouched as she poured a second glass. Then a third. It was almost 7 a.m. when she woke, fully clothed still, on the couch. "Shit." She grabbed her jacket and, leaving her car keys, pulled her bike out of the lean-to shed by her front door.

―――

"Morning, boss," Michelle said, as they both arrived by the station entrance at the same time. "Still on the keep fit drive?" She looked at the bike.

"What? Oh yeah. Gotta try, haven't you?" Rachel unlocked the chain and secured the bike.

"Forgot your helmet though. I should book you for that," Michelle joked. Her face straightened after a stern look from her boss.

"Save your booking sheets for the two shithead boy racers that nearly knocked me off down Scratton Road."

"That stretch of road is a nightmare, I know. Traffic really need to put some speed cameras down there."

Halfway down the corridor, what Michelle said finally resonated with Rachel. "What did you say about Scratton Road?"

"Huh?" Michelle replied. "About there being no cameras?"

"Yeah."

"Exactly that. Well, speed cameras, that is. There's a grainy CCTV one, but not one that registers speed. No good to you on this one. I don't know, drivers seem to think they can tear arse down there and they won't get done. Probably think that, because it's the road leading out of town, they can speed up."

They walked into the office and plonked their jackets down on the back of their chairs. "Get me the ANPR records and the footage from the CCTV cameras down Scratton Road. I want to see every driver that drove down there on the day Amanda said she got a message from her mum. And I need the CCTV from that pier in Prussia Cove."

"We have already looked through it. We couldn't see Diana."

"We're not looking for Diana this time. We're looking for Amanda."

Chapter 20

Michelle walked over to the far end of the canteen after finally locating Rachel, who was reading through her notebook. "You been hiding in here all morning?" she asked.

"Something like that. I'm avoiding the boss. I think we're close and I don't want her to pull us off the case. I figure if I stay out of her way then I can buy us some time. Anyway, find anything?" Rachel asked, looking up from her lunch.

"Yeah, we've finally got all the footage combined into one stream." Michelle pinched the bridge of her nose. "It's ready to view, if you are?"

"Lead the way."

Once sat in the viewing room, Michelle pressed the play button. Within moments a bus stopped near the pier at Prussia Cove, and a figure of medium build, wearing dark trousers and a purple hoodie, with the hood pulled up over their head, stepped off. Rachel looked at the time stamp.

"Pause it there, Michelle," Rachel said, scribbling in her notebook. "Now, hit play again."

The hooded figure continued to walk along the pier. When they reached the end, they appeared to look over the railing.

"There. Did you see?" Michelle said.

"Yeah, just rewind it though. I want to be sure." Rachel leaned closer to the monitor.

Michelle rewound the tape and they watched the clip again. Sure enough, the figure appeared to drop something over the end of the pier. Rachel checked the time stamp against the time Diana Walker's phone had connected to the mast.

"Pause it there. Zoom in. There. Clear as day."

Rachel sat back and smiled at Michelle, their suspicions confirmed. Although the close-up of the figure's face was pixelated, it was undeniable who it was.

"This will be enough to buy us some more time. Dig me out the press conference footage, Michelle. There's one more thing I want to check before I haul Amanda in."

Michelle did as she was asked. Once she had located the file she hit the play button.

"Damnit." Rachel slammed her fist on the table. "How the fuck did I miss that?"

"What?"

"Look at Amanda. When she asks Poppy for a tissue. Look closely."

Michelle replayed the clip over and over again until she saw what Rachel meant. "Her eyes. They're as dry as a fucking bone. Not a single tear."

"Why the fuck did I not spot that?"

"Don't beat yourself up. You're human. I didn't see it either. No one did. She's obviously a genius at being a fucking psycho. But one question remains."

Rachel nodded. "I know. Where the fuck is her mum?"

―――――

"You're going over to Amanda's house again tonight?" Mrs. Lovell said. "I know you're trying to be a good friend, Poppy, but we really don't like the effect this Amanda is having on you. You never drink, you never stay out and you definitely don't normally get warnings at work. Turning up three hours late and still smelling of alcohol, Poppy? That's not on."

Poppy ripped her jacket from the coat stand near the front door of her parents' house and scowled at her mother.

"She's my friend. She needs me and I'm old enough to do what I want."

Her mother's protests fell on deaf ears as Poppy slammed the door behind her.

———

IN THE SEMI-DARKNESS of the lighthouse basement, the group had sat around the table for five minutes staring at Amanda, who was making a blithe attempt at small talk. Her expression turned serious.

"So. You all know why I'm here. You've had long enough to discuss your answer. So, I will ask one more time." The group twitched. "Where is the burying place?"

Before any of the group could think of an answer, The Therapist emerged through his concealed panel door from his office behind. He glared at The Copper.

"I thought you were taking care of this?'

The Copper frowned. "Me? What you on about?"

"I sent you a message." The Therapist took out his phone, then swore. In his drafts folder, there was his message. "Never mind." He turned to face Amanda square on. "Mullion Cove. That's where the bodies are buried."

Amanda clenched her jaw. "In the sea? So, I'll need a fucking boat then. I guess that's where you, Mr. Fisherman, step up to help me."

"Fuck off, Amanda. You have the place, but that's all the help you're gettin'. That water's rough though, so I'd be careful. A novice sailor might drown." The Fisherman's words dripped with unapologetic menace. "I think the best idea for you is to let your mum go, swear 'er to keep it quiet, then we all get to put this fuckin' nightmare behind us."

Amanda snarled. "The best thing for you lot, more like."

The Therapist stepped forward. "He's right. If you say you felt traumatised by your dad's passing, and you made up some story about why you kept your mum captive, you may get a lesser sentence due to mental health issues. I can corroborate that with my patient notes on you. It's not a murder charge, Amanda. You'll avoid mainstream prison. You don't need to mention the other bodies. Yes, we all benefit, but you would too. If you'd only see sense."

———

Rachel pressed the call button, then swore, having to wait for the beep. "Amanda, this is Detective Inspector Morrison. I'd like to speak to you urgently. I went over to your house but there was nobody home. Please call me back as soon as you get this message."

"When she checks that message, I'll get the location of the phone," Michelle said.

———

Amanda looked down at her phone screen as the missed call message lit it up. "Fucking police." She turned her phone face down on the table.

"Come clean, Amanda," The Therapist said. "None of us will mention anything else you've told us. It's not as if we can't keep a secret, now, is it? Let your mum go. Kidnap isn't as bad as murder. You can still do the right thing."

"Which one of you is the one who cleans up the scene afterwards? Out of interest?" Amanda's voice was calm.

The Copper sat back in his chair and folded his arms. "Why?"

Amanda replied with a chilling smile. "Of course. It's you, isn't it? Because I plan on taking you with me when I dump my mother. You can scrub the boat afterwards, so there's no trace. My dad has a small boat. We brought it up with us when we moved here. It's ironic that my mum didn't want to sell it after my dad died, and now she's gonna end up in it. The police think my mum's topped herself anyway, so they won't be surprised if the body floats onto the beach if I do end up fucking up." She shot a withering look at The Fisherman, who looked as if he wanted to gut her like a monkfish right that second.

The Therapist leaned across the table. "But it's wrong, Amanda. Don't you see? This is all my fault. If only I hadn't got you all involved in my mission to rid the town of scumbags. I've created a monster with you, Amanda. It was never my right to bring justice to the town. I've been selfish, I know that now. I was trying to come up with ways to try and stop the pain of losing my daughter. But it doesn't stop. It's always there when I wake up and when I go to sleep. All I've succeeded in doing is bringing normal people into a world they should never have become a part of. A world of shame, torment and guilt. They wanted justice and they tried to do it the right way, but because I was grieving so much, I told them there was only one way, and that was to get that person eradicated by us forming a kind of chain where everybody had their own part to play. I admit, I was impressed and surprised that it went so smoothly. But at the end of the day, three people's remains are now at the bottom of the ocean, and that's because of me. I don't want to look out my window and know that there's another body out there too. I'm pleading with you, Amanda. I don't want you to do anything you will regret. We are both grieving for people we lost and loved very much. It sounds like the police are on your tail anyway. The walls are closing in, Amanda. But you can still take control as to how this ends."

After a few seconds of him finishing, Amanda began to clap. "What an impassioned speech. Have you been rehearsing that one?"

The Therapist lowered his head. "Amanda, please."

The group watched with bated breath. In front of them, Amanda seemed to be thinking over The Therapist's words. For a moment it looked as if she would agree, but as quickly as that hope rose, it was dashed seconds later by a sly grin that draped itself across her lips.

"Nope. Not interested. You forget, I actually get a fucking buzz from doing this. Did you not hear me in therapy? You, doctor, gave me a reason. A purpose. When I hear somebody's last breath, I get a rush from it. I can't explain it. And when I get away with this, I've got a couple of others I'd like to see at the bottom of the sea too." She pushed her chair backwards, the wooden legs screeching against the cold stone floor adding to the group's misery. "Or, if you want it your way, I'll do it on my fucking own, and you'll all go down with me. I don't give a fuck either way."

"Amanda, come back. Think about what you're doing. The lives you're wrecking," The Therapist called out, but Amanda's ears were deaf to reason. Adding insult to injury, she slammed the door shut behind her.

―――

"WHAT THE HELL do we do now? She's lost it!" The Gardener yelled. It had only been a few minutes or so since Amanda had left them in the basement, each person in a similar state of panic.

The Therapist stood bereft. He sat down and buried his head in his hands.

"We can't just let her sink us. Someone must have an idea," The Teacher piped up.

As if regaining his composure, and his senses, The Therapist looked directly at The Copper. "Come with me."

"Where are we going?" The Copper replied, refocusing his eyes.

"My house first to get Amanda's address. This ends. Tonight."

Chapter 21

"Amanda? Are you home?" Poppy called through the letter box. No answer.

She scrabbled in the darkness underneath a rock next to the door and picked up the spare key. After letting herself in, she walked into the kitchen and placed the key, her phone and a bag of shopping on the counter. Just as she began unpacking it, a crash underneath her feet startled her. Walking over towards the utility room, she saw that the washing machine door was open, the clothes from it already neatly hung up like they were when she'd left last time.

The crash came again.

Poppy looked down at the rug beneath her. "Amanda? Is that you down there?" She peeled back the rug and hooked her fingers around the silver ring on the hatch. Hearing another ominous crash, she yanked the hatch upwards and peered down into the blackness. "I'm coming down." She put a hand out to steady herself as she descended the first few steps, before locating the light's pull cord. "Sorry, Amanda, I didn't know you were ho-"

Moments later, Poppy saw the bricks of the cellar spinning around. With an almighty thud, she landed at the bottom of the steps in a heap. Lifting her head out of a cold puddle, she saw an upturned bucket. Next to it was the base of a chair. Poppy looked upwards to see a dirty figure tied to it. Bound, gagged and covered in wine splashes, Diana Walker's eyes conveyed an emotion that was completely confusing to Poppy. What should have been relief was translated into pure panic and sorrow. Realising she was lying in Diana's shit and piss, Poppy grimaced and struggled to sit up. The crashes now made sense, as all around Diana's feet were shards of broken glass from the wine racks she had rocked her chair into. Poppy brushed off the glass, then looked back up towards the light from the hatch. Her blood turned to ice when she saw the reason for her fall.

"Why the hell can't you stay the *fuck* out of my business?" Amanda growled.

A baseball bat, now splattered with red blotches from Poppy's cracked head, hung limply in her grasp.

———

"Too many people have gotten hurt. I caused this mess. I need to do the right thing now," The Therapist said over and over again as The Copper drove.

"We all got involved in this for our own ends, Rich. You can't keep blaming yourself." The Copper looked over at him for a moment too long, almost missing the turn off to Amanda's house. "Shit," he said, swerving at the last second.

"I need to ring that detective. We'll never get there in time." Baker called the number from the card Rachel had given him. He drummed his fingers against the car door as he waited for her to pick up. "Detective? It's Dr. Richard Baker. I didn't tell you everything about Amanda. She's dangerous. You need to get over to her house, now. We're still twenty minutes away. Her mother is in serious danger. What? Don't you see why there's been no sightings of her? Because she never left the house. I know you searched it, but not everywhere. I've only just remembered what Amanda told me a while back in one of her sessions. She was grounded once for stealing a bottle of wine from her mother's prized collection? Yes, that's right. Diana Walker had a cellar conversion when they first moved in. I think she's down there. It's the only explanation. Yes, she's alive. I think. But she won't be for much longer if you don't get there quick. Oh, and by the way, Amanda's father owned a shotgun. He left it to her in his will. I thought it best to warn you."

RACHEL HUNG up the phone and called for Michelle. "We need to get to the Walker house. And we're going to need backup."

"I'll call the local units," Michelle replied, picking up the phone. Rachel reached over and plunged her finger into the hook switch.

"We also need armed response units, at least two in case she really has got a bloody shotgun and this becomes a hostage situation."

IN LESS THAN TEN MINUTES, Rachel and Michelle had made the journey to the Walker residence, arriving just after two marked response units. Thankfully, both drivers had turned their flashing blue lights and two tones off well before reaching the address in accordance with Rachel's earlier instructions that all units responding were to make a silent approach. They also had the foresight not to park directly outside the address, so as not to tip Amanda off.

The four response officers looked towards Rachel for guidance as she alighted from the car. Holding up a finger for them to wait a moment, she rushed around to the boot to grab her personal protection equipment. As she donned her ballistic vest, she spotted Richard Baker and another man standing across the road watching them.

"Where the hell did they come from?" she asked herself, then turned to face Michelle. "Tell two of the uniforms to make their way around the back, but not to engage anyone until I've carried out a dynamic risk assessment. For the time being I want them to put in a visual containment. The other two are to go either end of the street and put up cordon tape. I don't want anyone but the Old Bill coming down this road until we know exactly what we've got."

As soon as Michelle had gone off to deliver her instructions, Rachel stormed across the road to confront the two men standing opposite. "Who are you?" she demanded, looking directly at The Copper, "and what are you both doing here?"

"DC Ben Taylor. From Helston CID. I was in the area and saw the sirens as I was driving down the highway. Thought I could help in some way?" He flashed his warrant card.

Rachel nodded. "Why are you here?" she demanded of Baker.

"I...I thought I might be able to help?"

Rachel's eyes narrowed as she considered this. Though, if he'd really wanted to help, he should have said something when she'd visited him. If he had, all of this could have probably been avoided. "For the moment, I want you both to stay back. I'm going to try and talk to Amanda before the ARVs arrive. Hopefully we can resolve this without anyone getting hurt."

"But before you do, I need to tell you the full story, well, the short version..." Baker said. The arrogant manner he'd had with Rachel previously was now completely gone.

"It'll have to wait."

Baker opened his mouth but Rachel was already halfway back across the road.

"Can you see anything through the window?" Rachel asked, pulling out her phone.

Michelle shook her head. "Nothing."

Rachel dialled Amanda's number. If she could hear Amanda's voice it might give her a good indication of her mental state. It rang until it went to answer phone. Rachel cancelled and tried again, only to get the same response.

"How long until the ARVs arrive?" she asked Michelle, who was monitoring her Airwave radio through an earphone.

"They were a long way off when we called for backup," Michelle said. "Latest ETA is five minutes. Also," she said, pulling a dour face, "I've just heard that Hargreaves is making her way down to the scene to take over as Incident Commander."

Rachel grimaced at that and then took a deep breath, forcing herself to consider the situation with complete detachment. Had Baker not mentioned the shotgun in his call to her earlier, her immediate reaction would have been to call upon a Personnel Support Unit, of Level II public order trained uniform officers clad in full riot gear, including NATO helmets, to carry out a rapid entry with long shields and secure the premises and everyone inside it. However, the possibility of a firearm being present—Rachel had checked with the licencing officer while en route and he had confirmed that she did indeed have a shotgun licence—cranked the risk assessment up from 'unknown' to 'high'. The fact that she had a licence didn't automatically mean that Amanda still possessed a shotgun. Even if she did, according to the licencing officer's notes on her application, the secure gun cupboard she'd claimed that it was locked in was located in the loft, which meant that she probably wouldn't have ready access to it and that it would take her a few minutes to get it out and load it.

They needed to establish an RVP at a safe distance away from the venue and await ARV arrival. An armed containment would then be put in place and the Authorised Firearms Officers would initiate contact and call the occupiers out in a controlled fashion. If Amanda was inside on her own, and she refused to cooperate, the situation would become a siege and the police response would be to just wait her out. The problem in this case was that Amanda wasn't alone; she had her mother as a hostage. A girl with mental health issues who had access to a firearm, and who was holding her mother—a woman she appeared to hate—hostage was potentially a recipe for disaster.

"I know it goes against all the rules, but I'm tempted to wander over there, knock on the door and just act normally," Rachel said.

"What? Are you mad?" Michelle replied, horrified at this idea.

"Think about it," Rachel said. "How many times have we been there recently? There's no reason for Amanda to suspect that Doctor Baker has tipped us off. The chances are that she'll open the door as normal and won't suspect a thing."

"Unless she opens it with a gun and blows a hole through your chest," Michelle countered. "I'm not worried about you but it would be a terrible shame to ruin that lovely designer blouse you're wearing."

Rachel smiled at that. "Call the guys covering the back," she instructed. "See if there's any sign of movement."

Michelle did this, talking quietly into her lapel microphone. She listened to the reply with a frown of deep concentration plastered to her face. She nodded and turned to Rachel. "All quiet; no sign of any movement at all."

By now, several more units had arrived, along with an ambulance containing ballistic injury trained paramedics. It was standard practice for one to be called to a firearms incident like this and the control room had automatically done so. An RVP had been set up at the end of the road and Rachel spotted Inspector Kay Peters, the Divisional Duty Officer for the late turn shift, padding towards her, using the building lines as cover.

Christ, this is turning into a fucking circus, Rachel thought, half hoping that she hadn't called all these resources out for nothing and half hoping, for Diana's sake, that she had.

"What have we got then?" Peters asked as she fixed her cap over her short blonde hair and straightened her ballistics vest.

Rachel indicated Amanda's house and gave her a quick run down.

"So, no gun has actually been seen?"

Rachel shook her head. "No, this is all based on information from her shrink. He reckons she's very unstable and on the verge of losing control. Plus, she has a shotgun licence and we have reason to believe the gun is on the premises."

Michelle stiffened and placed a hand on Rachel's arm, pointing towards the house. "Look."

Through the front window of the house, they saw Amanda walk casually across the living room, holding what appeared to be a glass of red wine in her hand. A moment later, she had vanished from sight and the light had gone off, leaving the house in darkness.

"For someone who's meant to be on the point of losing it, she looks pretty chilled out, if you ask me," Peters said, raising a questioning eyebrow at Rachel.

"I agree with your assessment," Rachel said. "I'm going to go and knock on the door. If the ARVs arrive before I get back, deploy them as usual, Kay," she said to the Duty Officer. "You have control until I get back or Her Royal Highness arrives to take over."

Rachel pulled her Airwave radio out of her pocket and twiddled the channel selector until she came to one of several back-to-back channels that officers could talk to each other freely on during stakeouts and other operations. "I'm going to be on channel five so I don't interfere with the main working channel," she said, plugging in the cord for her earpiece and then unwinding the cord. "Can you listen in case it all goes wrong and I need to shout for help? Keep me posted on what's going on out here. I'll call you forward as soon as I can."

"I think I should come in with you," Michelle said as soon as Rachel reached her.

"I'm not so sure about that," Rachel said. It was one thing for her to risk her own life, but risking the life of a junior colleague didn't sit well with her.

"She's used to seeing us together and besides, two on one might make Amanda think twice about doing anything stupid."

"OK. Get your Kevlar vest on. Be sharp though, if I need you. Understand?" She gave Michelle a knowing look.

"Copy that."

"Be careful in there, both of you," Peters said. "It's a lot of paperwork for me if you get yourselves shot."

Taking a deep breath, Rachel and Michelle began their walk up to the house. As they approached, they saw that the front door was open a crack. They stepped closer, their backs against the fence, mindful to try and avoid triggering the security light. Once at the front door, Rachel turned to Michelle. "Stay vigilant," she whispered.

Michelle clasped Rachel's forearm. "What are we going to do if she answers and she seems perfectly normal, bearing in mind that, if Doctor Quackface is right, she has a gun somewhere?"

"Whatever happens, we're going in under Section 17 to search for Diana, so as soon as I give the signal, let's restrain Amanda and cuff her for everyone's safety." Rachel patted her chest, feeling her hand thud against Kevlar plating. "Let's hope, if she does have a gun, she shoots us here and not in the head or the legs," she said with a devilish smile. It was a typical gallows humour joke brought on by nerves, but it got a smile out of Michelle.

Rachel raised her hand to push open the front door. "Hello," she called out.

There was no response. Inside, she could hear the TV playing. After exchanging glances with Michelle, she padded into the hallway.

"Amanda? It's Detective Inspector Morrison. Are you home?"

A crash from underneath her made her look over towards the utility room. As she made a slow track over there, using the wall as a guide in the darkness, a lamp clicked on in the living room.

"Hello, detective inspector."

Rachel spun round to find Amanda sitting in an armchair behind her. "Hello, Amanda," she replied, forcing her voice to remain calm despite her rising heart rate.

Something metallic in Amanda's hands glinted in the lamplight, causing Rachel's blood to run cold.

"What have you done to your mother, Amanda? Where is she? And why have you got a shotgun in your hand?" As she spoke, she surreptitiously pressed the press-to-talk button on the Airwave cord clipped to her jacket lapel.

―――

Outside, three shiny silver BMW five series estates in full Force livery glided to a halt at the RVP, signalling the arrival of the Armed Response Vehicles. Each car contained three Authorised Firearm Officers who were armed with Glock 17 9mm pistols and tasers. They also had access to two Heckler & Koch MP5 (SF) 9mm carbines and two Heckler & Koch G36C (SF) carbines that were secured in a gun safe inside the ARV's boot.

The senior officer amongst them, PS Lewis, came forward to find Inspector Kay Peters. "Alright, guv," he said. "What have we got?"

"Not sure at the moment. Maybe something, maybe nothing. Worst case scenario, we have a mentally unstable woman holding her mother hostage. Even if she hasn't got a gun, she will have ready access to kitchen knives and the like."

PS Lewis grunted. "The bloody DI shouldn't have gone

inside," he said. "That flies in the face of Force procedure and makes my job ten times harder."

"I know," Peters replied, "but what's done is done, and if you wanted an easy life you would have chosen a different career, wouldn't you, so let's just crack on, shall we?"

PS Lewis grunted. "I'll go and get my team ready," he said. "Call DI Morrison up and tell her to come out right now."

As he started to walk away, Peters shouted out, "Wait." Her hand had flown to the side of her head, where her earpiece was, and the colour had drained from her face.

"Rachel just transmitted on the back-to-back channel. I just heard her speak to Amanda and the last thing she said was, 'why have you got a shotgun in your hand?'"

"Bloody hell," PS Lewis exclaimed. He sprinted back to his team to get them ready for a rapid deployment.

Richard Baker and Ben Taylor had watched events unfold with bated breath. "We need to get in there. This is going to end in tragedy," Baker said, seeing the firearms officer rush off with a look of grim determination in his eyes.

"The side gate. We'll go round the back before the AFOs deploy," Taylor replied.

"But there are officers around there," Baker said. "They'll stop us from getting through."

Taylor pulled his warrant card out. "Not if I show them this and say DI Morrison sent us there, they won't."

"Put the shotgun down, Amanda. There's no need for this to end badly," Rachel said in an even tone as she heard Peters' voice in her ear, informing her that the ARVs had arrived and were getting ready to deploy. Rachel kept her hands in the air, and tried to remain completely focused on Amanda. "Michelle, why don't you go outside and wait for me there," she said. "I want to have a little chat with Amanda in private."

"Stay where you are. Both of you," Amanda said. "No one is going anywhere."

"OK," Rachel said. "But put the shotgun down in case it goes off accidentally and someone gets hurt." She squeezed the press-to-talk button, praying that Peters would hear and pass the update onto the AFOs.

"I don't think so, detective. If I put this gun down, it's all over. I'll be put away for a long time."

"And if you don't, and someone gets hurt, do you think the outcome will be any different?" She risked a glance over her shoulder to check that the curtains were still open. Thankfully, they were. Without making it obvious, Rachel shuffled a step to the left, taking herself closer to the wall by the door. She bumped into Michelle, who was standing by her side, forcing the confused constable to mirror her move. As she had hoped, Amanda took a step to her right to maintain the distance between them. This put her in full view of the window leading out to the street. The Authorised Firearms Officers would now be able to see her every move and would have a clear shot if they needed to take it. Rachel prayed that it wouldn't come to that.

"You think I care now? The game's up for me." Amanda raised the shotgun to point it straight at Rachel. Her voice bordered on the hysterical, and for the first time Rachel saw just how disturbed she really was.

"Amanda, *no*. There are armed officers outside. As long as you don't point that gun at anyone, they won't do anything. But as soon as you do, they will see that as a threat to life and act accordingly. Do you understand what I'm saying? They will have no choice but to shoot you dead. So, please, lower the gun for all our sakes."

Amanda shrugged. "You act like you are all so perfect, but you're not. You're pathetic and very predictable." The latter comments were directed over her shoulder towards the hallway.

Rachel and Michelle exchanged confused glances. Who was she talking to? Her mother, perhaps? Rachel wondered.

When Amanda spoke again, her voice was hard and cruel. "Come on out, you pathetic piece of shit. Surely, you didn't really think you could sneak up on me without me noticing?"

Rachel heard the hall floorboards creak as someone moved along them, and then she detected movement out of the corner of her eye. Nothing distinct, just a lighter shadow moving through the greater darkness that surrounded it.

"Come out and join us, Doctor Baker. Now that you're here, why don't you tell Rachel about our sordid little secret?"

Rachel turned her head to the side. Out of the darkness Baker and another figure emerged from the hallway. Internally she swore. "I gave you a direct order, DC Taylor, to stay outside," she said through gritted teeth.

"Sorry," Taylor replied. "Thought you might need some backup." He lowered his eyes from Rachel's scathing stare.

Amanda laughed. "How professional, DC Taylor." Her face straightened a half-second later. "Doctor Baker? We're waiting."

Baker looked thoroughly ashamed. "Will you put the gun down if I do?"

"Of course," Amanda replied. The tiny grin at the corner of her mouth made her words less than convincing. "As soon as Taylor over there," she glared at Ben, "admits his involvement too… Oh, I see…" she looked back at Rachel, closer this time. "You've got an earpiece in." Amanda's face turned murderous, almost a little panicked. "Take that shit out now."

Rachel moved slowly, taking great care not to antagonise Amanda, whose finger had crept onto the trigger of the shotgun for the first time. "OK. Amanda, see? It's just my earpiece. I'm not recording anything. Look, it's out now," she said, removing it. Holding it in her hand, Rachel had pressed the transmit button while she spoke in order to update the officers outside that she would no longer be able to hear them.

"No, you misunderstand me, detective inspector," Amanda said. "You don't need to record any of this. Why? Because *I* am. On my phone, here." She held up her phone. "I'm in control now."

"Rachel... Rachel, don't. For fuck's sake, she's taken her earpiece out." Inspector Peters fumed. She turned to the AFO team leader. "I don't like where this is going," she said. "Tell your team to be ready to move in if this looks like it's going tits up."

"They're ready," he assured her, looking around at the three officers who had taken up static cover positions around the front of the house. Two were leaning on the bonnets of parked cars directly outside the house, with clear lines of fire should they need to act. Clad all in black, they each shouldered a Heckler & Koch G36C semi-automatic carbine chambered to fire a 5.56 rifle round. It was an accurate weapon, and both men had informed PS Lewis that since Rachel had shuffled to her left and the suspect had moved to her right, they now had a clear unobstructed shot on the target.

PS Lewis lowered the binoculars he had been holding to his eyes and transmitted an urgent message. "Standby, we have two unknown males entering the room. The suspect currently has her weapon pointed at the floor between the police officers and the newcomers, but she now has a finger on the trigger. If she points that bloody thing at anyone and she looks like she is going to squeeze the trigger, you are greenlit to take action. Confirm my message, over."

Chapter 22

"THE GROUP WAS MY IDEA. A way of ridding scum from this town. It seemed like the perfect solution. When Amanda came to me for therapy, after her move here, we spoke at length about how she felt after her father's suicide. She blamed her mother, I knew that." Baker paced the living room floor, then switched his gaze from Rachel to Amanda. "All those crazy things you did, Amanda? Especially to that poor cyclist. Leaving him for dead after hitting him. They never found his body, the poor soul, but when you told me about how it intrigued you—excited you, even—I thought I'd found the right person to carry out my mission. If you could call it that?" He shook his head and looked back at Rachel. "I asked a psychopath to kill, then expected her to stop. How could I, of all people, not have realised the insanity of that?"

"I got a taste for it, you could say," Amanda chipped in.

"Richard hired a local fisherman to dump the bodies of those missing people. He knew a spot where the tide was just right and the depth was out of reach. I prepped and cleaned the scene so forensics wouldn't have a clue," Taylor admitted.

Amanda laughed, turning to face Rachel. "You have been round this house more times than I can remember, and have literally been standing on top of where my mum is. You're a fucking shit detective. And for a drunk, I'm baffled at you not checking out the wine cellar."

It was Rachel's turn to be surprised. "What do you mean by that?"

"Twice I've smelt alcohol on your breath when you've been round. And you drove here most times, so *you* ain't fucking perfect. I wonder what your boss would say if I told them that? I bet the plod you come with, Barlow, would verify. How the fuck can a copper come round here preaching about doing the right thing when you've at least twice been drunk driving?" Amanda shook her head and tutted in mock outrage.

Rachel's eyes remained fixed on Amanda, but she felt Michelle's eyes on her after hearing Amanda's accusation. "You're right, Amanda. I'm not perfect, nor do I claim to be. Anyway, we're not here to discuss that. We're here to sort this —." Rachel's raised voice was overshadowed by a ringing from the hallway.

After the outgoing message, the voicemail kicked in, and Mrs. Lovell's strained voice sounded. "Amanda? Are you there? Is Poppy with you? She said she was going over to yours with some shopping, but she hasn't come home yet. I've messaged her twice, but nothing. I'm worried. I'll try her mobile again. Please call me when you get this message."

Seconds later, a mobile phone vibrated on the coffee table.

"Where's Poppy, Amanda? That's her phone, isn't it?" Rachel said.

"She shouldn't have kept letting herself in my home unannounced. Do you have any idea how *sick* of takeaway dinners I am? It's her own fucking fault anyway. But DC Taylor, you should be happy your guys turned up when they did."

"Why?" Taylor replied.

"Because if they hadn't, you'd have to deal with a two-for-one down there." Amanda laughed.

"Is Poppy dead as well, Amanda?" Rachel asked, again

secretly squeezing the press-to-talk button as she had done periodically.

"My God, Amanda! What have you done?" Baker exclaimed, moving towards her.

"Stay where you are," Amanda growled, raising the shotgun in his general direction.

"Stop," Rachel ordered. "Baker, stay where you bloody well are. Amanda, please lower the weapon. If you point that gun at anyone, I can't guarantee your safety." Her voice softened. "Please, Amanda, no one has to die today."

Baker froze on the spot but he looked imploringly at Rachel. "There are two people down there, in God-knows-what state!" he yelled.

"I know," Rachel said.

"You may as well put that gun to your own head, Amanda," Taylor spat out. "You're fucking finished."

Amanda looked genuinely furious. "I did the job *you* were both too chickenshit to do. I took three people out, on your orders, Richard. And I have all of it on audio right here to prove I didn't do it alone. Oh, and one other thing, Richard. I taped our sessions where you said how much you could help me with my new obsession of watching people die. Just for back-up."

"Believe me," Baker raged back. "If I could change things, and report you to the police when you first told me about your depraved new hobby, I would do. Do us all a favour and pull that trigger against your own sick head."

"Get off your moral high ground," Amanda sneered. "I have no problem taking us all down, and you know I'll fucking do it." Her finger twitched on the trigger and the gun in her hand wavered between Baker and Taylor, not quite pointing at them but coming dangerously close.

Taylor glared back. "If they shoot you, we all win. Your mum, us, everybody else who is on your fucking hit list!" he yelled at Amanda. He looked across at Rachel as if he was seriously thinking about rugby tackling her to the ground and wanted her approval. Rachel gave a barely perceptible shake of her head, making it clear she wanted him to stay still.

"Hit list? I like that. Yeah, there's a few. It's like you read my mind. But I've been taping this since Columbo, here, came in." Amanda cocked the gun towards Rachel, but she had removed her finger from the trigger guard, the detective noticed. "So when I'm dead, they will hear about our little secrets, and Rachel being a drunk. I win either way, really."

"Amanda," Rachel pleaded, "look at me. Not at them, look at me." She waited for Amanda to do so. "You won't get out of here alive. You do understand that, don't you? By now, there will be several highly trained marksmen pointing guns at your head. The only sensible thing to do is lower the shotgun and let me help you."

Amanda snorted at the offer. "Time to get one shot off then, at least?" She looked at each person, one after the other, enjoying watching them squirm. "Which one will it be? The Copper? Bent fucking weasel that he is. Or The Pisshead Detective, who gets drunk before her shift, then drives around hungover? Jesus, no wonder you didn't solve this case sooner. You'll be the fucking joke of the force by the time my recording of this gets out. Or The Therapist. The man who brought me into this world and opened my eyes to all its glory. Hmmm. Eeny, meeny, miny—." As she reached Baker, she lifted the shotgun, her finger squeezing the trigger.

The glass in the front window shattered into a million pieces. Amanda dropped to the ground like a stone. Blood began to trickle out of a clean red hole in her forehead.

Rachel, like the others, ducked, cradling her head in her hands. Recovering, she rushed forward and stooped over Amanda, kicking the shotgun away from her hand.

"Suspect down, suspect down," she said, pressing the transmit button. Stepping over to Amanda's outstretched arm, she bent down to pick up the phone that had fallen out of Amanda's jacket. Just as she'd said, Amanda had the voice recorder running. Rachel pressed the stop button and pocketed the phone before checking her pulse. Amanda lay motionless, staring up at her through unseeing eyes. With a loud bang, the front door burst open and the sound of booted feet announced the imminent arrival of the AFOs.

Half a dozen heavily armed police officers stormed in, looking like ninjas and shouting their standard battle cry of "ARMED POLICE, ARMED POLICE, STAY WHERE YOU ARE AND RAISE YOUR HANDS!" Rachel ignored this and rushed straight through to the utility room, where she lifted up the rug by the washing machine. There she saw the silver ring of the hatch and pulled it up. Carefully, she descended the steps and found the light pull cord. Clicking it on, she saw Poppy lying on her side, bound and gagged. She was motionless. Lying in the blood from Poppy's head was a dog collar. She bent down to read the tag. *'Buster. If found, please return to Max Killick, 31 Heath Drive, Kynance Cove.'*

"Fucking hell, what a bitch," Rachel murmured. She rushed over to Poppy and checked her pulse. In the opposite corner was another figure, their head lolled to one side.

"Down here!" Rachel called, after hearing the paramedics inside the house. Within seconds they were rousing Poppy and putting her on a stretcher. Rachel stood over the figure lying on her side, still bound to the chair, and slowly, carefully, removed the blindfold. The figure opened their eyes very slowly and blinked into the half-light.

"You're safe now, Mrs. Walker," Rachel said, removing Diana's gag.

"Thank God," Diana replied.

"WHAT ARE you going to do now?" Ben Taylor asked after Rachel arrived back outside the house. "About the tape."

Rachel glared at him. "The right thing, of course."

Taylor clenched his teeth. "We're all fucked then, aren't we?"

Rachel strode away, after seeing Hargreaves beckon her over.

"What the fuck, Rachel? How did we not know her mother was in the fucking cellar? The press is going to crucify us for this." Hargreaves' face remained calm, in spite of the fury she clearly felt.

"I'm fine, thank you for asking," Rachel replied. Hargreaves' eyes nearly bulged out of her head at the impudence of that, but it shut her up for a few seconds. Rachel sighed. "It's going to take a few days to process the crime scene and collate all the evidence," she said. "There's a lot we still don't know yet, but I'll have an interim report on your desk outlining the basics ASAP."

"You had better do," Hargreaves hissed back. "There are already half a dozen reporters here, circling like vultures, and they won't stop pestering me until I throw them some scraps. I want to see you in my office first thing in the morning, understood?"

"Ma'am."

"Good. Now gather everyone who was involved in this clusterfuck together and get them back for a hot debrief. Then I want them all to write the most comprehensive set of fucking notes they have ever committed to paper. You'll have to attend the Police Incident Procedure with Inspector Peters and the AFOs involved in the shooting. I'll let you know where that's going to be held as soon as it's confirmed. In the meantime, I'll smooth things over with the reporters after I get them on the right side of the fucking cordon." She looked over at them and flashed them a murderous glare. "But there'd better be one mother of an explanation for all of this."

As soon as Hargreaves stormed off, Michelle rushed over to Rachel and threw her arms around her. "You had me worried there," she said when they finally broke apart.

"I don't mind admitting that I was worried too," Rachel replied.

Chapter 23

HARGREAVES EXPECTED to see Rachel sat in front of her, ready to brief her fully at 9 a.m. Without fail, she'd arrived on the dot. She looked and felt like shit, having had hardly any sleep, but she was still just about functional thanks to consuming her body weight in caffeine.

"Right, I'm all ears. Begin," Hargreaves said as she leaned forward in her brown leather office chair and glared at Rachel, who stifled a yawn and cleared her throat.

"Amanda Walker was having therapy due to grieving the loss of her father who took his own life and it was coming up to the anniversary of his death. Last night, she disclosed to her therapist that she had killed a cyclist six months ago, after hitting him with her car. Told him she had stood over him and watched him die. She had got a thrill from it."

"Charming," Hargreaves said. "Carry on."

"Amanda had been drinking and taking drugs at the time. The cyclist was reported missing and presumed dead. So the case went cold. Baker made a welfare call to me last night, as he had reason to suspect she was about to hurt her own mother too, whom she blamed for the death of her father. So, myself, Baker and his friend, who is a serving police officer from Helston CID, called round to the Walker residence.

Amanda was there, and quite brazenly told us she was willing to kill us, as she had already killed three other people."

"The unsolved cases we're getting shit for?"

"Yes ma'am. Amanda heard rumours about them being arseholes, so she thought they would be ideal victims. She killed them in cold blood. It was sport to her."

Hargreaves clasped her hands together and made a steeple with her fingers.

"Ma'am, Amanda set all of this up with her mother. She kept her mum captive, while pretending at first she'd been kidnapped, to divert us away from suspecting her. She then orchestrated this subterfuge of her mother supposedly planning to take her own life."

"Why such an elaborate plan, when she could have just done what she did with the other murders and got away with it?" Hargreaves asked, her brow wrinkling.

"Because the other murders were in some way justifiable. There were rumours spreading about the moral fibre of the three that went missing, so in some way Amanda must have thought it was OK. But when it came to her mother, she couldn't do it straight away. She had to make her suffer first. Drag it out, so her mother could feel the pain and suffering Amanda was feeling over the death of her father. Somehow, using suicide as a cover story seemed fitting, I guess. Karma for her mother, you could say."

"Sick young woman."

"So, she told us she takes out her dad's fishing boat, and goes out to sea around Mullion Cove, weighs the bodies down and dumps them over the side. Her friend Poppy must have disturbed her last night and ended up being tied up down in that cellar too. She was no doubt going to be Amanda's fifth victim. We also found the collar of her ex-boyfriend's dog down in the cellar, which was reported missing the morning after he broke up with her. He got freaked out when, during a night of rough sex, Amanda cut him deep with a knife to the point the bedsheets were soaked in his blood."

"Did he not report this? That's GBH. We could have had her for that, got a search warrant for the bedsheets, then investigated that house a bit more."

Rachel swallowed, knowing Hargreaves was correct. "The boyfriend didn't want to make a statement. Anyway, as I passed the desk sergeant on the way in, ma'am, I was informed that the badly decomposed body of an IC1 male has been recovered from undergrowth at the side of Lincoln Road."

"Relevance?"

"That's the road Amanda's hit and run happened on. The male has been identified by his driving licence and security tag on the bicycle next to him as a Mr. Declan Short. Married. Newborn twins at the time."

"Bollocks," Hargreaves muttered.

"I'm going to speak to his wife straight after this."

"Leave out the bit where she watched him die slowly, won't you?" Hargreaves advised.

"Ma'am."

"So, to sum up?"

"In conclusion, we've solved one high profile case, three cases in the public eye, and one we didn't know about. Amanda also searched the victims on Google and Facebook *before* they went missing, therefore showing premeditation. The culprit is dead so no lengthy court case wasting more taxpayers' money," Rachel said, knowing she was saying all the right things.

"A great result, Rachel. Well done. We might get some peace around here, finally?"

"Thank you, ma'am." Rachel got up to leave.

"Oh, and Rachel," Hargreaves said. Rachel turned. "I'm glad you didn't get hurt in all of this."

Rachel recoiled, surprised by the lightness in Hargreaves' voice.

"Me too, ma'am."

"One last thing," Hargreaves said as Rachel pulled open

her door. "It seems a lot for a young slip of a girl to do all alone. I mean, how did she get the bodies to the boat? Were there any accomplices?"

Rachel froze. She'd been dreading that question. She waited a second before answering. "No. She acted alone."

Hargreaves' eyes narrowed. "OK. Great work. I'm glad you didn't listen to me when I said to give up on the case."

Rachel smiled and closed the door behind her, not entirely sure if Hargreaves' last comment was made in jest or not.

Outside the station, as Rachel was making her way to her car, Ben Taylor jumped out in front of her.

"For fuck's sake," Rachel exclaimed, pressing her palm against her chest.

"I just need to know what's happening and if I'm going down?" he said, rubbing his stubble. "What did you do with her mobile phone?"

Rachel stared at him. "I must have accidentally dropped it as I was walking near the cliff edge this morning when I listened to the audio files she'd taped."

Taylor sighed with relief.

Rachel leaned into him and snarled. "I'm not protecting you, you ignorant shit. You should have known better than to get involved in all of this. If it wasn't for all the other people caught up in this, I'd have your fucking badge."

"And what about the group? What should I tell them?"

"Go back to your manor, DC Taylor. I don't want to see you in my town ever again. Understand? Now, if you don't mind, I've got to go and tell a wife that the decomposing corpse of the father of her twins has just been pulled out of a ditch."

RACHEL DROVE AWAY from the Short residence, feeling close to tears herself. Telling a wife her husband wasn't coming home had been hard enough, but seeing her holding two six-month-old babies in matching pyjamas made it near on unbearable. She sat in her car after stopping at the end of the street and broke down in long overdue floods of tears.

It was almost half an hour before she composed herself enough to drive on. Her mind now made up, she drove to the first address she had written in her notebook after her final visit to Richard Baker. She wanted to see for herself who the members of this group were. She knew she should do the right thing.

Arriving in Penzance, she pulled up across the street from a smart, detached house about a mile from West Cornwall Hospital. Grabbing her jacket and warrant card, she pulled at the handle of the car door just as the front door of the house opened and a middle-aged brown-haired lady emerged carrying a small child. She put him down on his feet and kissed his head, then ruffled his hair.

"Bye, Granny, I'll see you in a bit," the little boy yelled as he ran to the outstretched arms of his mother.

"Thanks, Mum! What would I do without you?" the dark-haired woman called back to the house.

"Love you both," the middle-aged woman replied, blowing a kiss and waving them off.

Rachel watched the scene unfold, then clasped her eyes shut.

"I can't do this," she whispered to herself, pulling her hand away from the car door. Without a second thought, she pocketed her warrant card, started the car engine and set off. She knew she should have arrested all of those involved. But it didn't feel right, not after she learned more about the cases from her last meeting with Baker.

Curious to see the others involved, she set her satnav to the next address she had in her notebook and arrived in front of a gorgeous cottage, with perfectly landscaped gardens. There, her decision not to arrest any of Richard Baker's group was reinforced further by the scene of tranquillity before her. A fit looking man with short dark brown hair was holding a glass of water to a man in a wheelchair's lips. They looked completely lost in each other as the first man wiped a few stray droplets from the second man's mouth.

The final address was a similar picture of domestic bliss. On the front lawn of a terraced house in the suburbs of Helston, a man was sat with his wife and a teenage girl playing Twister. Their laughs as one fell over made Rachel smile.

"They've all suffered enough," Rachel said under her breath. She picked up her phone and dialled a number she had neglected from ringing for far too long.

"Mum, hi. It's me. Fancy lunch? My treat?"

Epilogue

"Call for you, boss," Michelle said as Rachel sat at her desk.

"Who is it?"

Michelle made a face which told Rachel it was best she didn't keep the caller waiting.

"This is Detective Inspector Rachel Morrison."

"Detective Morrison, this is Superintendent Graham Jenkins up at Merseyside Police. I heard about your excellent work down in Cornwall and was wondering if you've ever thought of a change of scene?"

"Sir?" Rachel replied, confused.

"We have a position just opened up at Merseyside Police, in Liverpool. I spoke to your super down there, and now all those misper cases have been sorted out, we wondered if you'd like to come up here and join us on an investigation we've got going on. We could do with a fresh pair of eyes on it."

"A change of scene?" Rachel repeated. *Could be just what I need*, she thought.

The decision had been an easy one in the end. With Adam still not returning her calls, and the dull boredom of very little to investigate in a sleepy town, now she had cracked the Walker case, Rachel had taken a few days to mull it over with her mother, but they had both reached the same conclusion.

Her last day was the Friday before she was due to start up in Liverpool. Michelle hadn't spoken to her properly since Rachel had told her.

"Hey mate," Rachel said, walking up to Michelle with two glasses of orange juice.

"Alright," Michelle replied, taking one glass.

"Come on, this is supposed to be my leaving do. You've had a face like a slapped arse all week."

"I'm pissed off at you for leaving me with Vinegar Tits over there," Michelle riposted, pointing over at Hargreaves, who was standing outside her office.

"She's a pussycat really. You'll be her new star player now, with your promotion. You didn't even tell me you were taking your exam. But DC Barlow does have a great ring to it. I'll even give you my desk organiser, how about that?" Rachel bumped her shoulder into Michelle's.

"You'd better come and visit. And if you pick up a scouse accent, I'll arrest you myself."

"I promise I won't," Rachel replied, crossing her heart.

"I bet your new partner's going to be shit too. Just saying."

They burst out laughing and clinked glasses. "To new beginnings," Rachel said.

Hargreaves raised her arms to call for hush. Michelle nudged Rachel and leaned in. "Speech time. Good luck."

———

Rachel unlocked her car and dumped a massive pile of presents and cards on the passenger seat. As she was about to sit down, Hargreaves called her back to the police station entrance.

"Yes, ma'am?"

"I've just had a call from Dave Connolly. Otherwise known as Drunk Dave?" Hargreaves watched Rachel as she waited for a reaction.

"Is he still banging on about lights in the sky?"

"Out to sea, actually. Adamant he'd seen them a few weeks ago and wanted to know what we were doing about them."

"He thinks they're aliens, ma'am."

"No, he doesn't. Not anymore." Hargreaves walked over to Rachel. "He's been doing some research. He gave me the exact make and model of the fishing vessel he believes the lights belong to. He also gave me the dates he'd seen it out there."

"Ma'am?"

"The dates match with the dates the people Amanda murdered went missing." Hargreaves waited for that to sink in with Rachel, who remained silent. "I thought Amanda only had a little rowing boat? With an outboard motor at best."

Rachel gave a nervous laugh. "Ma'am, with all due respect, are we seriously going to take the word of a man who is hardly ever sober, over a full confession to myself, another police officer and Amanda's own therapist? I mean, she'd even researched the victims online prior to them going missing. We have her hard drive down in evidence. She had motive, means and the opportunity." Rachel stepped forward to Hargreaves. "And you have all cases wrapped up nice and neat."

The merest glimmer of a smile formed at the corners of Hargreaves' tight lips. "Hmmm…so it would seem."

Nodding, Rachel turned away and headed back to her car.

"But something else, Rachel…" Hargreaves called out, causing Rachel to stop in her tracks.

"Ma'am?" Rachel replied, turning around.

"I've also had the lab report back from the boatyard near Amanda's house. The starter motor on her dad's boat was broken." Rachel felt her legs wobble slightly. "And the force of the current out by Mullion Cove would have torn that hull to shreds. It would have been suicide for Amanda to sail out there alone. Well, *row* as it would seem now." Hargreaves' eyes bored holes into Rachel's face. Before she could think of what to say, a voice called out behind them both.

"Superintendent Hargreaves." John Stretton, MP for Kynance Cove South, rushed over to them and reached out his hand for Hargreaves to shake. "I just wanted to congratulate you and your team on a fantastic result for the community. All those disappearances solved. Thank you for not giving up. If you don't mind, I'd like to have a photograph with you? The paper said they'd run the story tomorrow." He leaned into her. "And it will look great for my approval rating."

As he rushed away back over to the press party by the flagstone steps at the entrance, Hargreaves looked sidelong at Rachel, who smiled. "Well, I guess some things will have to remain a mystery. Won't they?"

"Ma'am," Rachel replied.

"Best of luck, DI Morrison. Keep in touch," Hargreaves said. She took a deep breath and strode over to the press pack.

Returning to her car, Rachel sat in the driver's seat and began sifting through the cards again. As she started the car, she noticed a small white piece of paper tucked underneath one window wiper. She opened the car door and reached for it and read the typed message.

Heart racing, she felt her lungs tighten, Rachel spun around in her car seat. There was nobody to be seen. Her blood like ice, she looked down at the message again.

I know what you did. It was a great cover up. But don't worry, it's our little secret.
For now…

WE DON'T SPEAK ABOUT MOLLIE

EVERYBODY KNOWS
WHAT YOU DID...

BOOK 2
IN THE
DI RACHEL
MORRISON
SERIES

EXCEPT YOU

VICKY JONES
AND
CLAIRE HACKNEY

FREE FIRST CHAPTER FOR YOU!

Now you've finished reading *The Burying Place*:

Want to know what happens next?

Read the prologue to Book 2: ***We Don't Speak About Mollie*** NOW!

Prologue

THE LITTLE BOY ran as if seconds from death. As he squelched through the mud as fast as his thin, short legs could carry him, the wind on the heather-coated Scottish moors jabbed its spiky claws into the soft skin of his face. It was pitch black in every direction, the sodden ground beneath his mud-splattered Nike trainers the only certainty as to what lay ahead. The last light he could remember seeing was the amber glow of the taxi's interior light. "Car won't make it up that dirt track in the dark. Not with those waterlogged potholes," the driver had said after driving him from the tiny train station in Crailach village. "But head straight up for about a hundred and fifty yards after the cattle grid, and you can't miss the farmhouse."

Icy cold sheet rain hit his skin like needles the second the boy had gotten out of the Volvo, matting his curly brown hair to sharp, dripping wet shards across his forehead. Finally, fifty yards after he'd stepped carefully over the slippery cattle grid, his longed-for destination was in sight. Almost crawling the last hundred yards, he collapsed exhausted at the front door of a cottage situated in the middle of nowhere. The tiny fragment of moonlight that peeked through the only crack in the storm clouds above glinted off the windscreen of an old tractor parked in the front yard.

Blinking through the rivulets of water running down his frozen face, the boy staggered up the driveway to the black-painted oak front door of the farmhouse and hammered on it. He hopped from foot to foot and wrapped his arms around himself as he waited for someone to answer. After what felt like an age, a light illuminated the window to the side of the door.

"Who's banging on my door at this time of night?" a sharp female voice called from behind the door.

"N-n-n-n-n-an," the boy said, his teeth chattering uncontrollably in his mouth and rattling like Scrabble tiles in a bag. "It's me. Robbie."

The door opened and a woman, easily into her sixties, appeared in the hollow. She was wrapped in a thick navy blue dressing gown and holding a lantern torch. She shone it unapologetically in the boy's face, causing him to flinch as his small brown eyes reacted to the bright light. He lifted his arm to cover his face and lowered his head.

"That's nay possible. My Rab's only a bairn. Can nay be more than ten." The old woman reached out a bony, callused hand. "Put yer arm down, ween. I can nay see yer face."

"It's me, Nanny Morag. I swear down," the boy said, sniffing. He lowered his arm and stared at her, his brown eyes now adjusted to the light that was being shone in them. The old woman let her wrinkly blue eyes inspect his face and nodded.

"As I live and breathe. It is. What in God's name are yer doing up here on yer own, so far from home?" Her eyes wide, she looked behind him and all around, looking for a vehicle.

"Something really bad's happened, Nan," was all Robbie could squeeze out of his freezing cold mouth.

Now visit Amazon to continue reading *We Don't Speak About Mollie.*

WE DON'T SPEAK ABOUT MOLLIE

EVERYBODY KNOWS WHAT YOU DID...

EXCEPT YOU

BOOK 2 IN THE DI RACHEL MORRISON SERIES

VICKY JONES
AND
CLAIRE HACKNEY

What if everybody knew what you did, except you? The Killer in Kynance Cove mystery has been solved, but haunted by the aftermath, DI Rachel Morrison is in need of a change of scene. After accepting a secondment from Cornwall to a brand new Task Force in Liverpool, she gets stuck in immediately. One day, a new, mysterious case is brought to her attention by Katie Spencer, a distraught young woman with a harrowing childhood secret.

The DI Rachel Morrison series

The Nurse. The Teacher. The Gardener.

You have motive. You have means. Do you take the opportunity? Three innocent people from completely different walks of life are presented with an impossible decision. DOWNLOAD FREE: www.hackneyandjones.com

The DI Rachel Morrison series

Book 2: We Don't Speak About Mollie

What if everybody knew what you did, except you? Seconded up from Cornwall to a Task Force in Liverpool, DI Rachel Morrison has a mysterious case brought to her. Haunted by her past, Katie Spencer seeks answers, but a familiar face tells her a story that completely destroys her world. Together with DI Morrison, Katie pieces together the fragments of her memory. But is knowing the truth a blessing or a curse? And just who exactly is Mollie?

Also by Vicky Jones and Claire Hackney

Chloe - A prequel to Meet Me at 10

What if a life-shattering family tragedy forces you to completely rethink your future? Destined for a different path in life, twenty-year-old Chloe Bruce's world is shattered after a tragic accident on her father's plantation in Alabama. Suddenly thrust into the limelight, as the new heir to the Bruce family business, she is sent off to university to study and equip herself with the knowledge needed to succeed her father. But not everything in life can be learned from a textbook, as Chloe realises when she meets Mia… DOWNLOAD FREE: www.hackneyandjones.com

Also by Vicky Jones and Claire Hackney

Shona: Book 1 - A prequel to Meet Me at 10

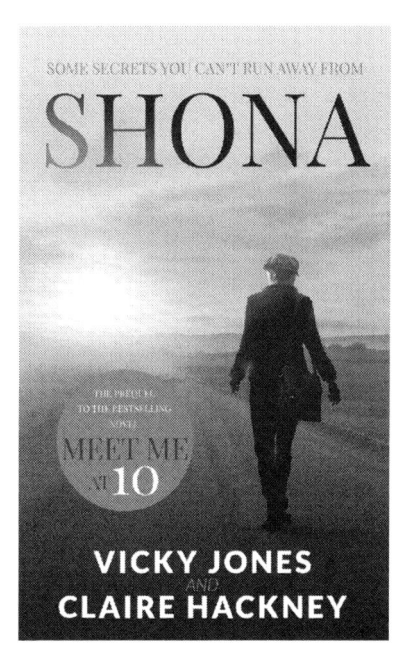

Everyone has a secret. Hers could get her killed…
Mississippi, 1956. Shona Jackson knows two things —how to repair cars and that her dark childhood secret must stay buried. On the run from Louisiana, she finds shelter in the home of a kindly old lady and a job as a mechanic. But a woman working a man's job can't avoid notice in a small town. And attention is dangerous…

Also by Vicky Jones and Claire Hackney

Meet Me At 10: Book 2

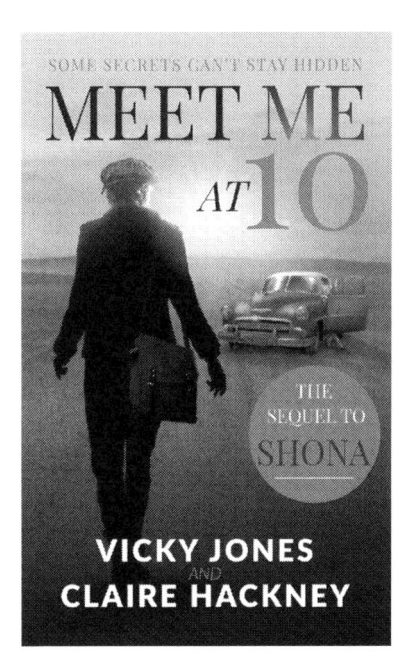

Four lives inextricably linked. Will tragic events part them forever? Shona Jackson is on the run again, forced to flee Mississippi. Arriving in Alabama, to continue her journey to safety, she convinces Jeffrey Ellis, the wealthy co-owner of a machinery plant, to give her a job. But when Chloe Bruce returns from college and is introduced to the workforce, there are devastating consequences for all those involved.

Also by Vicky Jones and Claire Hackney

The Beach House: Book 3

New town. New life. Old enemies. With the past and present colliding and threatening their future together, can Shona protect her new life and the lives of those closest to her?

Join in!

If you would like to receive regular behind-the-scenes updates, get beta reading opportunities, enter giveaways and much, much more, simply visit the site below:

http://hackneyandjones.com

Acknowledgments

This book has been a passion project, but we couldn't have done it without all our friends and family supporting and believing in us every step of the way.

Special mention to Sharon Atkinson for being so supportive in the writing group where it all started.

Many thanks to all of our beta readers, and for all the amazing support we've received from our **Hackney and Jones** Facebook group.

Our Team

Virtual Assistant:
Erin Hodgson
writehandwomannz@gmail.com

Book Covers by:
WooTKdesign
wootkdesign@gmail.com

Edited by:
Gary Smailes
Bubblecow.com

Proofread by:
Melanie Bell
inspire.envisioning@gmail.com

Printed in Great Britain
by Amazon